FALLEN

E. PRYBYLSKI

FALLEN. Copyright © 2022 E. Prybylski. All Rights Reserved. No part of this book may be used or reproduced in any manner whatsoever without written permission except brief quotations. For information, contact Insomnia Publishing.

Bilblical quotes were taken from the New International Standard Version.

Cover image designed by Angel Leya.
https://www.angeleya.com/

www.insomnia-publishing.com

ISBN: 978-1-7344305-6-1

To Jason, my muse, my beloved, without whom none of this world would exist.

To my mother, whose dedication to reading to me as a child taught me to love books.

To myself. You don't believe in yourself as much as you should. This is proof. You can do it.

If you enjoy this book, please leave a review wherever you purchased this book. Reviews help others find authors' books. It's more important than you know.

CHAPTER 1

The first thing I remember was the rain. I'd never felt anything like it before, and the sensation of it landing on my skin fascinated me. The scent of wet earth filled my nose. I stirred, sitting up and coming to realize I lay in something of a depression that must have been formed by my impact on the earth in what I later learned was Boston, Massachusetts.

As my senses cleared, I realized I could hear voices. And I understood them, though I knew they weren't speaking the language I knew best.

"Do you think he's okay?"

"Should we call the police?"

"Probably."

"Where did he come from?"

"He? That's not a man."

"Sure it is."

A small crowd had gathered, and more were coming, fascinated perhaps by my abrupt appearance. As I studied them, still trying to put the pieces together, a man wearing dark blue clothing distinct from all the others strode over to me. "Hey, you okay? What the hell happened?"

I opened my mouth to reply, and, to my amazement, English came out. "I… fell." My head felt like it was spinning, and I lay back down. My neck and chest throbbed and burned with pain I didn't entirely understand. I lifted a hand to touch it, finding my skin slick. When I pulled my fingers away, they were coated in red. Blood.

The sounds around me faded, and weariness overtook me. I closed my eyes. They felt so heavy. The voices around me continued, but I could no longer make out the words.

"When they could not find a way to do this because of the crowd, they went up onto the roof and lowered him on a mat through the tiles into the middle of the crowd, right before Jesus. When Jesus saw their faith, he said, 'Friend, your sins are forgiven.'"

A soft, low voice spoke from somewhere to my right. I knew the words, but when I tried to speak the next verse, it came out in my native tongue and rather slurred. I opened my eyes, smelling something sharp and astringent in the air. Looking around, I had no real understanding of where I was. I had never seen a hospital before, after all. To my right sat an older man. His features suggested human, but not all metas are immediately obvious, or so I have learned. His short, red hair was threaded through with gray at the temples, though his gray eyes remained lively and warm. Hunched as he was, I couldn't guess at his height beyond the vague awareness that he was shorter than me.

"Ah, you're awake." He had an accent of some kind and sounded quite different from the others. "S'a good thing. Heard you came in here all torn up with no one to come and visit you. So I figured I'd sit with you. If you don't mind, o' course."

I sat up a little, groaning as my left shoulder pulled. "I do not mind."

"Good, 'cause I'm here anyway. They didn't give me your name, by the by. I'm Father John Carver, one o' the chaplains here at Mass General."

"Mass general what?" I frowned.

"Hospital. Mentioned you were havin' a bit o' trouble rememberin' things."

"I am not struggling to remember."

"If you say so. What's your name?"

"Cassiel. My name is Cassiel."

Father John Carver nodded a little. "Nice to meet you, Cassiel. Do you remember how you got in the park? Police officer told the people here you said you fell."

"I did, yes. I fell." The words felt like razors in my mouth.

"Where'd you fall from?"

"Heaven, Father John Carver."

That gave him pause, and he cocked his head to the side, brows rising. "Heaven, you say?"

"Yes." I looked around the room. "I hurt." Everything ached. The injuries to my jaw, neck, and chest burned and throbbed, and I reached to touch the area.

Father John Carver took my hand, his fingers so much darker and more weathered than mine. And bonier. His bones stood out against his skin, wreathed in veins, a mark of his age. "You should leave the stitches alone for now. Don't need to make it worse, though you shouldn't be hurting. Let's see if we can't get them to give you something for that." He squeezed my hand.

The warmth of his skin fascinated me, and I turned my hand over, wrapping my fingers over his, staring at where we touched. It was such a simple thing, I knew. Those of the world were creatures of touch, and it was one of the primary ways they communicated. The Father had created them that way.

Even with my interest in the sensation, it was strange to be touched, and it set me a little on edge despite being in control of the situation. I didn't really understand why, and I studied the point of contact as if it would provide answers.

He didn't pull away and just let me keep hold of his hand, his smile never faltering. "All right. You can have that for now. Though I'll need it back eventually."

"Yes." I traced the back of his hand with my thumb, feeling the bones and tendons under the surface. He felt so delicate. So fragile. I could have crushed him without effort, which made him feel all the more precious. "Father John Carver?"

"You can just call me Father John. Most people do. What is it?"

"Where do I go when I leave this place?"

"You're not in danger of dyin', Cassiel. But I'd like to believe—"

"No, Father John, I meant when I leave this room. How long am I to stay? Where do I go?"

He frowned. "Home, I'd hope."

My throat tightened, and I looked away. "I cannot go home."

"Mind tellin' me why?"

I did mind. My voice shook. "My Father has cast me away." Father John's smile faded then, his bushy brows drawing together and mouth turning down at the corners. A frown. I had upset him. "I am sorry. I did not mean to upset you, Father John."

"Sounds like you've been through a lot." His gentle words echoed the way he squeezed my hand. "When you leave this place, you can come to the church with me. You can stay there for a while until you find your feet again. How's that sound?"

I smiled a little and nodded. "Thank you." I sat upright and cross-legged on the bed, the strange garment I wore exposing my back to the cooler air of the rest of the room. I found it uncomfortable and fidgeted.

A tall, willowy young man wearing scrubs entered the room, his delicate facial structure and leaf-shaped ears marking him as elven. Perhaps fae, since they were so similar in structure, and the species were related somewhere back in the mists of time. I didn't linger on that curiosity long because he smiled and walked over to me before asking a number of questions about how I was feeling and what I remembered. While I must not have answered all of them correctly—if the expression on his face was any indication— he seemed satisfied enough and had a brief conversation with Father John, to which I paid scant attention.

A hollow sort of quasi-pain had begun in my abdomen, and I touched a hand to it, frowning. "There is something wrong."

My words drew the attention of both men. "What are you feeling?" the elf asked, his body posture displaying a readiness to act I didn't think the situation warranted. When I described the sensation, he relaxed but gave me a quizzical look. "You're hungry, probably. I'll have the kitchen send something up."

"This is what hunger feels like?" While the various texts with which I was familiar mentioned hunger and thirst many times, I had never had a point of reference to really understand what that meant. Logically, I knew it meant I needed sustenance, of course, but knowing of its existence in a clinical way and experiencing it were quite different.

I didn't see their expressions since I was wrapped up in my own thoughts surrounding the whole affair and stared down at the blanket covering my legs. I heard the elf ask Father John if he was certain he wanted to take me back with him.

Father John dismissed the idea of doing anything else. The elf left the room, presumably to provide me with some food. Father John then reached over and touched my knee, which made me jump. "Hey. You went somewhere for a moment."

"I have been here the whole time, Father John." I frowned, unsure how he could have forgotten me, and I looked around to confirm I had not, in fact, moved from the bed.

The warmth of his laughter filled the air around us, and I looked at him. "My child, my child, I meant to say you were thinkin' o' somethin' other than what we were sayin'."

My cheeks felt warm, and I touched them, frowning. "Why is my face hot?"

"You're blushing."

"What does that mean?"

Father John cocked his head. "It means you're a little embarrassed."

"I am?"

"You're the one blushing. You tell me."

A sigh left me. I had so much to learn. "Maybe a little."

"So, you say you fell from Heaven. That would make you, what, an angel?" His tone suggested skepticism, though I could see him trying to keep it off his face. I knew even those of faith might not believe, so I shrugged.

"I am a seraph. The angel Cassiel, they who preside over one of the gates of Heaven."

"Sounds like you're pretty important."

"All things have their purpose. That was mine. Perceived value is irrelevant."

Father John nodded slowly. He didn't believe. If he had, he likely would have reacted more strongly. After all, there is a good reason most angels introduce themselves by saying, "Be not afraid." Whether he believed me or not made little difference in the scheme of the world, but part of me ached for reasons I couldn't put a finger on.

Some of what I felt must have shown on my face because Father John patted my shoulder. "Don't think on it too long,

Cassiel. Everythin' must feel new and strange to you right now, but we'll get you set to rights. Don't worry on that score. For now, just rest up, eat when they bring you your food, and I'll get a space ready for you at the church. All right?"

"You are leaving?" Worry rose in me at the idea. I didn't want to be alone, and while he didn't believe me, having someone—anyone—treat me with kindness was something I couldn't sacrifice so quickly.

Father John lifted his hands. "Only for a little while. I'll be back." He stood with a tired noise and stretched out his legs like they bothered him, hobbling a couple steps before his strides lengthened and his back straightened.

Once alone, I spread my hands, staring down at them. I felt naked without my sword, without my station, and now without Father John.

———

Some time later, a polite, smiling dwarven woman brought me a tray of food and showed me how to sit the bed up so I could eat more comfortably. Her beard had been done up in a number of braids with shining beads amongst them. It suited her round face and sweet smile perfectly. She also explained how to eat, though she seemed flustered by the question. I must have appeared very strange to her, looking back. But she taught me patiently enough, and by the time I'd finished eating, I at least understood the use of the utensils. They were simple, after all, and despite my lack of experience with them, I was no newborn child still learning to use their hands.

Dwarves are, in general, a short, stocky people with glorious beards that they never cut. Their religion tells them that, much like Samson, if they do so, they are breaking a vow to their gods and will lose their strength. While some modern dwarves eschew this notion, many still adhere to the old ways and begin growing their beards in childhood.

The food itself didn't thrill me, nor did the act of eating, largely because microwaved chicken and overcooked rice wouldn't excite anyone—even if it was the first meal of my life. Apparently, it was between meal times, so the kitchen wasn't ready, and that left me with a microwaved meal. I didn't know the difference at the time. The food at least sated the discomfort I had in my abdomen. After that, I discovered needing to use the bathroom, which presented its own problems. Those I won't regale you with.

CHAPTER 2

When the day of my discharge came, I didn't have any clothes but the tattered, bloody remains of the robe I'd fallen in, so they found me clothes from the donations the hospital took for people in a similar situation to mine. A nurse helped me figure out what size I was and taught me how to dress. In retrospect, I appreciate her kindness now more than I did then since, at the time, I didn't much understand why I needed to wear two sets of clothing on my lower body. She didn't bother providing me with a bra since I am almost utterly flat-chested.

She had clucked a little over needing to provide me men's sizes since I am built larger through the shoulders and chest than most women and narrower in the hips. Eventually, she fitted me in a pair of dark blue jeans and a gray t-shirt she said looked like they matched my eye color well. However, she lamented a little bit that I looked so masculine in the outfit since she thought I'd look quite pretty in something that suited me better. I didn't much care how I looked and was content to not upset people by being nude.

In build, I am about six feet tall and have virtually nothing for breasts, although I possess a fair amount of muscle through my chest and ribs. As a seraph, I was one of Heaven's warriors, so I was designed with that in mind. My hair is black, and my eyes are a dark blue, resembling the color of blue sapphire. I have an aquiline nose, a strong jaw, and very pale skin due to where I spent my eternity stationed—there was very little light, so I needed no melanin to protect against the sun's rays.

By human standards, I am told I am quite attractive, though I have learned that most denizens of the world have trouble discerning my gender due to my neutral appearance. Before I fell, I don't think I had a gender. Or, if I did, it wasn't something I had ever been conscious of, which is common enough among angels.

Some possess genders while others have none. Of course, some angels and other members of my brethren, being beyond the scope of mortal comprehension, lack bodies resembling anything capable of possessing a gender.

With me dressed and discharged, I stepped outside the hospital to sit on a bench and wait for Father John, who told me he would be there. I stared around at the streets, the people, the life, and soaked it all in with a mixture of anxiety and elation. On one hand, there was so *much*. After an eternity spent alone in silence and calm, the frenetic pace of a major city was too much for me to process. On the other hand, there was so much! I saw so many things I didn't understand but wanted to. I felt the sunlight on my skin and the breeze through my hair. I smelled the exhaust from passing cars and the tantalizing scent of a street food vendor nearby selling hot dogs slathered in chili. The sights and smells and sensations held me on a knife's edge of too much and not enough.

Father John showed up in the corner of my field of view, smiling and dressed in what I would come to know as his usual attire: jeans and a button-down shirt with his clerical collar at his throat. He was an unassuming man with a brilliant smile and a spring in his step.

Extending a hand to me, he led me to the nearest T station to take me to the church where I would be staying. I didn't much enjoy the trip on the subway. There were far too many people, and while I was able to put my back to a wall, I had trouble watching them all at once. I didn't understand my need to know everything going on around me, only that it was very much a need. The subway itself, though, was a brilliant creation, and I tried to focus more on my interest than the simmering anxiety. The ride didn't last long anyway, and soon, Father John led me off the train and to the church he shepherded.

St. Mary's Church in Boston is a modest stone building on Westview Street beside a cemetery of the same name. It houses perhaps a hundred parishioners on a Sunday for each of their three services. None of it is top-of-the-line, but it has the comfortable, well-used feeling historical places of worship often develop. And, of course, the acoustics of the church proper are incredible. There are moments when I can close my eyes and listen to the singing and almost imagine my siblings of the celestial choirs joining in. Which, I am certain, was the intent of the designers, even if they didn't really know it at the time.

The building itself is a bit run down, needing more funding than it has been given since it is located in a less-than-affluent area of the city. Most of the people who fill it don't have a great deal of means to donate, but it is well loved nonetheless. The community works hard to do maintenance and pay for its upkeep. When the roof leaks, some of the local workers patch it rather than having it taken out of the church's meager funds, for example.

Beside the church sprawls a graveyard that long since has stopped receiving bodies. Father John said they had run out of capacity sometime in the 1950s, but most of the cemetery was from the Civil War, whatever that was. That said, the church itself and the cemetery are both true consecrated ground, which was a bit of warm relief to me since it is my understanding that such things have become rare in the modern world, or so Father John said.

After showing me around the place, Father John sat me down in a chair in his office and leaned his arms on the desk, watching my face. "Now, Cassiel. If you are going to stay here, I'll need your help. Once you're healed, I mean."

Father John's office in the church was a relatively small room directly off the sanctuary, which he also used as a ready room for his preaching. It had a desk, a couple chairs, a couch, and far too many bookshelves crammed into the small space. The furnishings were old, maybe even antique—and the computer also fit that description. Though he seemed to keep it working through a combination of threats and cajoling.

I nodded. "Of course, Father John. It is mine to serve." I smiled a little at him. It felt good to be of use to someone, somehow, so I found myself eager to do the work he mentioned.

"We have a number of regulars here, and everyone shares work in cleaning, cooking, and so on. We all work together. I imagine we'll eventually figure out who you are so you can—"

"I know who I am, Father John. I am Cassiel."

He closed his eyes and let out a slow breath. "Of course." It didn't take someone with empathy born of magic to see his disbelief. I understood. For all the world contained many wonderous and fantastical things, being confronted with absolute proof of Heaven itself was more than most people could manage. Beyond that, I certainly didn't resemble what he must have imagined angels looked like.

Father John opened his eyes again. "On that note, knowin' who you are, I mean, what pronouns do you use?"

Of all the things he could have asked me, that caught me off guard. "Pronouns?"

"Aye. He, she, they, xer…" He rattled off a number of them. "I ask because there's so many creatures in God's world. Some of 'em reproduce with pollen and dancing, so…"

"I do not know." I frowned and looked down at myself. "I believe I am female? That is what the nurses told me, anyway."

"All right then. But you don't have to be just what someone else says you are." He nodded. "So, do you think you can help with the chores?"

"I am… Cassiel. All other words are just… markers for communication. They do not matter to me. I am willing to help, but I do not know how."

Father John raised a brow. "What *do* you know?"

I opened my mouth to respond but hesitated. I could tell him I knew how to fight and destroy demons and act as a guardian. That would be true. But at the same time, I doubted it would be beneficial to the conversation. Instead, I shook my head. "Not much that is useful."

"Well, just because it may not be useful here to us now doesn't mean it isn't useful." Reaching over, he patted my hand. "I'll teach you what you need to know, and we'll figure this out together."

I smiled a little and nodded. "Thank you, Father John."

"Ain't no harm in not knowin' a thing. And we'll get you up to speed in no time. Are you feelin' well enough to help me to get some things done?"

The ride on the T and the new environment had left me with anxious energy to expend, despite the deep ache in the wounds I bore. I nodded.

He rose. "Come on, then. Let's get to cleanin'. If you need to stop, you just tell me."

We spent the next hour working together. Father John taught me how to sweep, mop, and dust. But before long, the stitched wounds on my neck and chest were pounding with pain, and it must have shown on my face because, though we weren't finished with the chores, he had me lie down on the couch in his office while he puttered about behind his computer.

I did as he suggested and sighed as I tried to rest, but we were soon disturbed by a sharp knock on the door. In my half-awake state, I sat bolt upright, groping for a sword that wasn't at my hip as I turned toward the sound.

Father John frowned at me. "Easy, Cassiel. That's just the door." He turned his attention toward the door and lifted his voice. "Come in."

The door swung inward, and a man in a strange chair entered. I noticed first that he had no legs from the knees down and that the chair had wheels. The sight of it struck me as a brilliant innovation and also profoundly sad at the same time. Everything else about him registered as secondary in that moment since I had not met anyone in a wheelchair outside the hospital.

He had chestnut-brown hair, a strong jaw, and warm brown eyes with faint crow's feet around the edges of them. His upper body carried a great deal of muscle, which compensated for the fact that he had no legs below the knee and used a wheelchair to get around. At the time, I didn't understand what about his bearing appealed to me, though I later learned he, too, was a soldier, which accounted for it.

"You are injured?" I asked.

The man, who had been about to say something to Father John, lifted a brow at me, his brown eyes looking rather sharp. "What gave it away?" he asked, the penetrating look remaining despite the smile he offered.

At the time, I didn't realize how rude I was being, and so I didn't try to censor myself. "You do not have legs."

He glanced at Father John. "And who is this?"

Father John sighed a little, rubbing the bridge of his nose, which caused his glasses to wiggle some. "This is Cassiel. She's a new resident here. What can I help you with, Jim?"

Jim looked away from me and rolled over to Father John's desk, pulling a folder from his lap. "Just dropping off some committee reports about the Clean Sweep project. And apparently meeting your new friend." He spun toward me. "You're Cassiel?"

The Clean Sweep project was one of Father John's many community outreach programs. He'd been working on it for years, or so he told me later. The whole point was to clean up various parks and such around the city to give the poorer communities safe places for their children to play. It also was trying to help discourage drug use by giving children and teens after-school programs to attend and putting money into local sports teams and such. Father John was passionate about it and talked my ear off about it more than once.

"I am Cassiel. Why do you not have legs?" The notion of being without them fascinated me. He certainly looked healthy enough otherwise.

"Cass," Father John interjected, "you canna just ask people things like that. It's rude." Him shortening my name confused me some, but I didn't mind it, so I didn't speak up.

My brows drew together, and I frowned. "I am sorry. I do not mean to be rude."

Tilting his head one way, then the other, Jim studied me for a long time without saying anything. "It's all right. To answer your question, I lost them in a war I fought in some years ago."

"You were a soldier?"

He nodded.

"I was also a soldier before I fell."

"Fell?" Jim raised a brow.

"From Heaven."

Jim exchanged a look with Father John before returning his gaze to me. "I see. Well, you're here now. If you were a soldier, then maybe you can help me out some. When you're feeling well enough to." He gestured to the stitches and bandaging down my neck. "I help soldiers figure themselves out. Maybe I can help you, too." Jim smiled some and offered me his hand.

I didn't understand what the gesture meant and awkwardly mirrored it. He must have realized I had no idea what I was doing, but Jim shook my hand firmly. "It's nice to meet you, Cassiel. Welcome to St. Mary's."

CHAPTER 3

fter meeting Jim, I spent the next few hours asleep on Father John's couch. The fatigue of the fall, healing, and trying to sort all this out overwhelmed me, and I didn't know how much time had passed until I felt something touch my shoulder. I jumped and grabbed for it, my fingers closing around Father John's wrist so tightly, he hissed through his teeth.

My eyes opened, and I looked up, recognizing him before I let go of his wrist, which was already starting to bruise. "Forgive me," I said, guilt pooling in my gut. That was an emotion I had already come to understand. "Did I harm you?"

"No, no. I didn't realize you were so jumpy," Father John said, shaking out his hand. "Now I know not to wake you up like that. I was going to tell you to come with me. It's time for dinner."

My stomach growled some in response, and I frowned at it. "I ate not long ago."

"Three times a day plus snacks, Cassiel. Come on." He grinned, stepping back from the couch to let me get up. "Besides, you're healin', which means you need extra."

I stood, discovering myself somewhat dizzy. I hadn't expected that and frowned but regained my footing swiftly. Seeing that, Father John gently shooed me out of his office and shut off the light to guide me to wherever there was food in this place.

The immediate darkness in his office gave me pause, and I stared at it. "How did you dim the sun?" I asked, not having really noticed the overhead lighting and, in my folly, assuming he had the window open.

Father John just stared at me for a second and flicked the light switch again, turning the lights on. I watched him do it. Then I tried it myself when he gestured to me to do so. I turned the lights off and on a few times with a grin. It was the small discoveries that excited me back then.

While I knew he must have been somewhere between irritated and amused, Father John let me play with the switch before taking my arm. "Come on. Let's get some food in you," he said, leading me through the sanctuary of the church and outside where we walked to one of the outbuildings.

Father John opened the door and let me inside first. I walked through and into the kitchen of what I would later learn was the soup kitchen and shelter that St. Mary's operated on the premises. Through generous donations of money and work, St. Mary's had the guts of an industrial kitchen. While a lot of the equipment was on the older side—most of it donated or bought from restaurants either upgrading or going out of business—it all worked.

"Dust," Father John said from behind me, "do you have room for one more?"

A large man with mottled green skin and tusks jutting up from his lower jaw over his lip spun and gave Father John a look. "Can they cook?" he asked, looking me over from head to toe. He was almost six inches taller than I was with a similar hairstyle to Jim in that his black hair was shaved nearly to the scalp on all sides and a touch longer on the top. They also had a similar set to their shoulders. Something in me recognized him as an orc, one of the tusked races.

There are three races categorized as the "tusked": orcs, ogres, and trolls. Orcs are about the same height as humans, but they're built broader and usually have green or gray skin. Ogres tend to be taller by a fair margin. Trolls are bigger still.

"No, she can't," said Father John, emphasizing the 'she' a little.

"Well, then I'll feed her. She can learn when she's less beat up," Dust said. He then met my gaze. "Sit down, and we'll get you fed. Can you help clean up afterward?"

I frowned, considering how I felt. "I am willing to try."

"Good enough." Dust nodded once. "Well, grab a seat." Dust turned toward someone else in the kitchen and barked orders.

While the words were English, I didn't understand why he would put shoes "up" someone's donkey.

Before I had a chance to ask, Father John nudged me out of the kitchen and into the main room. We walked over stained, old tiles and sat down at a folding table in a pair of plastic chairs that I was worried would not hold us. Around us, people slowly filtered into the space. As more and more of them crammed around the round tables and settled in, the room grew louder, and I could feel my heart rate rising as I tried to keep watch of them all at once. While I hadn't liked the T, this was somehow worse. At least on the T, my back had been to a wall.

I tried to regulate my breathing and keep my discomfort from showing on my face as we waited. More people came in, stuffing the room, and I lost count of them as they all chattered, laughed, and some yelled over one another. Without explanation, I stood up and retraced my steps through the kitchen and out the back door we'd come through. I didn't yet know the layout of the building, so I followed the route I did know.

Dust was still in the kitchen, getting food put together when I went through, and I felt his gaze on me but didn't say anything to him, either. I just needed to be out where it was quiet. As soon as I stepped out of the building, I felt like I could breathe again, and the tightness in my chest eased a little. I wasn't alone long, though. The door opened behind me, and I spun toward the sound, again reaching for a sword that no longer rested at my hip.

The big orc lifted one hand. "Easy, easy." He pointed toward a leaning plastic table with a few chairs around it. "Just going to put your food there. Not a big people person, I take it?" Despite the gruff manners he'd displayed in the kitchen, he spoke in an even, calm tone as he addressed me.

"I do not know what that means." I sat down at the table where he set the plate.

Dust sunk down in one of the other chairs. "It means you don't do well with crowds or people," he answered. "You looked like you were about to panic when you came through the kitchen. Father John was hot after you, but I told him I'd take care of it. I know a soldier having a moment when I see one."

I nodded, not touching the food just yet. "How did you know?"

"How did I know what?"

"That I was a soldier."

"Because I was one. Also, I've spent a lot of time around homeless veterans. You learn how to read 'em. Me 'n Jim have put a lot of work into the veterans' programs here. You met Jim yet?"

"The man with no legs."

"He'd be pissed if that's how you remember him, but yeah." Dust nodded. "I get the feeling you're not from around here or... Well, whatever it is, it's probably better to think about Jim for who he is rather than whether or not he's got legs."

"I have only met him once, so I do not know who he is. I have only just... arrived." I didn't know how to express it otherwise.

"Ah. Well, there's three people who keep this place running besides Father John. Me, Jim, and Eirlas." He said the last name like *eye-er-lass*. "I manage the kitchen, Eirlas manages the shelter, and Jim oversees the support groups and runs a couple himself."

"I see." I poked at the food, discovering that the noodles covered in red sauce was delicious. I didn't know it at the time, but when he wasn't volunteering at the shelter, Dust ran a kitchen at one of the fancier restaurants in the city. He has never said which. Once I started eating, my hunger returned, and I devoured the meal he'd given me.

Dust smiled a little. "You met Eirlas yet?"

I shook my head.

"I'll introduce you to him after we clean up. Unless you're hurting too much." He gestured vaguely toward my bandages.

The few hours of sleep had done a great deal to help, and the food seemed to provide energy I didn't quite know was missing. "I am willing to help."

"Good." Dust nodded. "Best thing for us is to keep busy. Don't sit around thinking too much. It'll take you down paths you don't want. I'm going to head back inside. Come in when you're ready, and I'll show you the ropes."

"Thank you."

Dust grunted. "We look out for our own. Leave no one behind. That includes you. Take a few minutes, then come in." He stood and nodded once before heading back inside.

I took a little while to let my meal digest and allow the last of the fear to subside. During that time, Father John joined me, checking in since I'd left so suddenly. I told him I was going to help Dust with the dishes, and that seemed to please him. He smiled some, the wrinkles around his eyes deepening.

"Good, Cass. We all work together here, but don't push yourself too hard. If you need to rest, say so. Working together doesn't mean killing yourself for it, all right? When you're done, come to the rectory, and we'll get you set up for the night on my couch. Tomorrow, we'll help you find your place here." He pointed to a small, two-story building resembling the appearance of the main church. It had to have been built around the same time to have such similar architecture.

I nodded. "All right. Thank you, Father John."

He patted my shoulder in a comforting manner as he passed by me, though the contact still felt foreign after so long without. It wasn't that I hated the touch, but it felt strange and somewhat uncomfortable.

When I had calmed enough, I took my plate inside, and Dust put me to work washing dishes. For all he barked at everyone equally, me included, he took time to show me how to do it properly and seemed content to keep half an eye on me while I did both to ensure I did it right and, I suspected, make sure I was neither panicking nor overdoing it.

I worked until the work was done. When I finished, I realized I was more tired than I would have expected for doing so little. Dust patted my shoulder—another person touching me that day—and jerked his head toward the door out front. "C'mon. I know you're tired, but I want you to meet Eirlas before you go. It won't take long."

I looked warily at the door. The kitchen only had five of us in it, which was tolerable since I could track everyone. But the idea of going back into that crowded room again made my chest tighten.

"Everyone's mostly gone. I've got your six," Dust said as though able to see into my head, but I had no idea what having my six meant at the time. That said, I nodded and took a deep breath, walking out into the cafeteria.

As Dust had promised, it was mostly empty. A few people milled around, cleaning tables and the floor, but the rush of people I had seen earlier was gone. Dust led me over to a shorter, slender elven man with pale skin. He wore a button-down t-shirt over another shirt with some kind of logo on it, and tattoos covered his forearms as well as on the side of his neck, and a teardrop sat under one eye. I had no idea what any of them meant, but the extent of them gave me pause.

He was talking to a young woman who I guessed was also an elf. They spoke rapidly in a language I didn't understand, but from what I could glean from their body language, they were discussing something important. The young woman had mousy brown hair, wore a large pair of glasses, and was dressed in slouchy clothing several sizes too big, but at least it looked comfortable.

"Eirlas," Dust said, waving to the smaller man.

Eirlas turned to look at Dust and nodded once before speaking in rapid tones to the girl again. She glanced at Dust and I with a shy smile before she headed off, vanishing out the front doors.

Despite his rather fierce appearance, Eirlas's smile was warm and honest. "Hey, man. Sorry. Mary Beth is staying with us again. Her father's..." Eirlas trailed off, expression angry. It took him a moment to compose himself, and he drew a deep breath before opening his eyes again. He gave me a look—more assessing than judgmental. "Newbie?"

"This is Cass. She's just arrived here today. Father John's been helping her find her feet."

Eirlas offered me his hand like Jim had, and I remembered the ritual, so I took his hand and shook it. "Welcome."

"Eirlas manages the shelter here."

"Shelter?" I tilted my head in confusion.

"We give people who don't have a home a place to sleep and eat," Eirlas explained without hesitation.

"People like me." I nodded.

Eirlas smiled a little. "People like you." He glanced up at Dust. "She looks dead on her feet, man. You might want to get her to Father John's." His attention returned to me. "It's nice to meet you, Cass. We'll talk more soon, but you look like you need rest."

Dust put a hand on my shoulder. "I'll get her over to the rectory. See you in the morning, Eirlas."

Eirlas smiled at the orc. "See you."

Dust shadowed me across the church campus to the rectory and, as promised, Father John let us in. He led me through the small kitchen into an equally small living room and pointed to the couch where he had a pillow and blanket set up for me. The couch looked comfortable, but to be honest, the floor also looked comfortable at that point. I lumbered over and lay down, too tired to take in more details than the presence of a blanket.

Father John and Dust had a brief conversation in low tones before Dust left and Father John came over to tuck me in.

"Sleep well, Cassiel," he said, making sure the blanket covered me well. He then left the room, and I fell into a deep sleep.

CHAPTER 4

The next morning, I woke when sunlight streamed across the floor and into my face. My neck and chest hurt far less than they had, and I had slept well. It still felt strange to lie down and not move for eight hours at a time. Even if it was what my body demanded.

I sat up and felt the urge to stretch, so I did. Again, something new. I had only been on the Earth for about three days now, but learning to listen to my body's demands made sense to me. Also, with them being demands, I didn't have much of a choice but to obey them. Needing to use the bathroom had me wandering uncertainly through the lower floor of the house until I found it.

The rectory's lower floor had a small kitchen with old, uneven cupboards; the living room I had slept in, which Father John had crammed full of comfortable-looking but mismatched furniture crowded around a fireplace; a small office (which, contrasted to the rest of the space, was a disaster of books and papers); and a tiny bathroom that looked as though someone had tried to squeeze a sink and shower into what was probably a supply closet or pantry when the rectory was built.

When I finished in the bathroom and came out, a sleepy Father John stood in the kitchen, putting coffee on. He wore a long flannel robe over a set of pinstripe pajamas and stood a little hunched. As soon as he noticed me, he gave me a weary smile. "Good morning."

"Good morning, Father John." I bowed my head to him some. "When do I begin working?"

He blinked a few times and tilted his head. "Usually after breakfast, child. We'll get you a change of clothes, too. And we should change the gauze on your stitches and make sure they're all set. I have the antibiotics they sent you home with on the counter here. Let's eat. You can shower, then I'll take a look at the stitches, and we'll go from there. But first? First is coffee."

"What is coffee?"

For the first time since we'd met, Father John looked genuinely offended. He then went on in great detail about the wonders of coffee and how it was God's gift to productivity, which he extolled the virtues of. When he made me a cup of it, I had to admit it was good, but I didn't get the boost from it that he described.

He made breakfast for us consisting of fried eggs, toast, and slices of fried tomato. When we finished, he showed me how his shower worked, pulled a fresh bar of soap out of the closet, and left me to it with a warning not to let the stitches get too wet. When I stripped off my clothes and removed the bandaging, I studied the ragged claw marks in the mirror. They went from the left side of my jaw down my neck to my chest, and while they appeared mostly healed, the marks remained. And itched, I realized as I looked at them. The stitches holding them shut itched like crazy, but I refrained from scratching them. I doubted it would be helpful, and I'd been told by multiple people not to mess with them.

After my shower, I dried off and put on my underwear and pants, stepping out into the kitchen. Father John glanced at me, blushed, and cleared his throat. "Ah, oh. Well. I take it you're ready for me to take a look at the stitches, hm?" He covered his apparent surprise with an awkward smile.

"Yes. I believe the wounds are healed." I sat down at the small table Father John had up against the wall.

He walked over and gently touched my chin to turn my head so he could study the injuries. "You're one of the fast healing sorts, I take it."

"I am an angel of battle, Father John. I must heal quickly."

He made a noncommittal noise and dropped his gaze, looking anywhere but at me. "Well... I think you may be right about these being healed, but we'll see what Jim has to say about it before we do anything else. That said, you can leave the gauze off until then if you prefer."

"I did not like the way the tape felt."

"Well, then we'll leave it. But put a shirt on."

I sighed, not really understanding why he was so flustered by me not wearing one, and I fumbled my way into the garment. "Better?"

He looked my way again. "Yes. Now, I'm going to take a shower, and we'll head over to the church and see what we can find for you to do." Father John smiled and headed into the bathroom I had vacated, leaving me alone at the table to drink a second cup of coffee. When he finished showering, he headed upstairs and returned fully dressed in jeans and a gray button-down shirt with a clerical collar at his throat.

We left the rectory and headed over to the church, where Father John led me into the church offices, situated in an outbuilding near the shelter. The small campus of buildings that made up St. Mary's church included the sanctuary, rectory, shelter and soup kitchen, and the administration building, which also held the gathering rooms where the small groups met as well as Sunday school classrooms. Jim's office sat on the first floor of the administration building off the main hallway near the wheelchair-accessible door leading into the shared parking lot with the sanctuary.

When we found Jim, he was hard at work on his computer and held up a finger when we walked in. Father John nodded, and we waited patiently until Jim lifted his head and gave both of us a smile. "Good morning, you two. What can I do?"

Father John closed the office door. "I was wonderin' if you could take a look at Cassiel's stitches. They look ready to come out to me, but... I fully admit you know more about this than I do."

Jim glanced at me. "All right, well, let me get my kit. I'll be right back." He moved from behind the desk and to the door, letting himself out while we waited.

"He's got some EMS training," Father John said as though that explained anything. My confusion must have shown on my face because he continued, "Jim took some medical classes since we sometimes have emergencies here, or people like you who would have trouble gettin' to the hospital to get help."

"Ah." I nodded.

A few minutes later, the door opened, and Jim returned with a satchel in his lap. "You can step out if you want, Father John." Jim gave me a smile, and I awkwardly returned it. "I'll take a look at things for you, and we'll decide if the stitches are ready to come out or not."

"They itch," I said by way of explanation.

Father John patted my back. "I'll be just outside, unless you'd prefer I stay?"

"I do not mind." I started undressing, and Father John scuttled out the door, closing it behind him.

Unlike the priest, Jim didn't seem bothered by me removing my shirt and set the bag on the floor, pulling out a small kit in an olive drab bag and donning a pair of gloves from a different package. "I'm going to have to get a little close to see what I'm doing well. That okay with you? I'm not going to touch anything I don't have to."

I shrugged. "I do not understand the fuss. You may do what you need to."

"Some folks are skittish about people without clothes, like the good father out there." He gestured to the door. "And others don't like having them off in front of others. I'm just trying to be respectful."

As he promised, it didn't take long. The stitches were ready to come out, by his estimation, so he wiped the area down with sterilization wipes and deftly removed them with a tiny pair of scissors and a set of tweezers. There were more of them than I had realized, but when he had finished removing them, I sighed in relief. The itching was gone, and I could move my head without feeling them pull.

"Thank you." I tugged my shirt back on, and Jim started cleaning up.

"You're welcome. Those are some nasty marks you got there. Father John said you just left the hospital, what... yesterday?"

I nodded. "I heal quickly."

"I can see that. Well, hopefully, we don't need to test it often, hm?" Jim smiled at me as he finished cleaning up.

I opened the door for Father John. He thanked Jim, and they had a brief talk about some church business before we parted ways. From there, Father John started teaching me about the various jobs that needed doing around the church. He showed me how to clean floors and bathrooms and turned me over to Eirlas for instruction on how to tend to the needs of the shelter. Then, in the evening, Eirlas passed me off to Dust in the kitchen to help wash dishes and clean up before and after dinner was served.

CHAPTER 5

It took me about a year to learn the basics of how to function in the world—or at least within the confines of the church. I'd soon taken over the bulk of the church's janitorial work in exchange for food and shelter. It wasn't that Father John would have hurled me out on the street if I hadn't done it, but he emphasized the importance of trying to "get me on my feet." I didn't understand why he called it that, since I was already standing, but I came to understand he meant to help me make my way in the world. Part of that was encouraging me to dedicate myself to some form of work. Even if it wasn't beyond the walls of the church. During that time, I had also come to accept touch more readily. It was, I learned, a large part of communication between people here. That said, I was only comfortable with a very few people putting their hands on me, though I had grown comfortable enough to shake hands during the passing of the peace at the church. I'd also endured the inevitable hug from several of the parishioners who preferred such methods of greeting.

I had gone out with Father John a number of times to purchase things for the church's use, and he'd taken me out to a bar with him a couple times a week. He'd told me it was so I could practice being in the world outside the safety and security of the church, but I suspected it might've been because he wanted to drink.

The bar we usually went to was a small Irish pub a short walk from the church. While I still didn't enjoy being in crowds of people, I had to admit it had helped some to go out with Father John and spend time among them. The pub was narrow and deep with low lighting and dark wooden fixtures. The whole place seemed to drink light despite the hanging pendant lights everywhere. Father John said it reminded him of the pubs back home, so he'd settled on this particular watering hole as his preferred haunt.

Today, we'd come in to warm up after having walked a fair distance to let Father John meet with someone regarding his Clean Sweep project. I hadn't been in the meeting and didn't know who the person was, but it had been at a nearby church as most of his meetings were. While it was early autumn still, the temperature plummeted as soon as the sun went down. He sat across from me with a glass of Guinness, his back to the room, and his gaze focused on the frothy surface of his drink. He'd had a couple of those rather large glasses ("pints" he called them) and had grown quiet.

"You need a drink," he said, abruptly lifting his head.

"I have ginger al—"

"No, no. A *drink*. Something with an umbrella."

"Why would I want a drink with an umbrella in it? Are those not too big to fit into a glass?" I frowned, trying to comprehend how one would even *fit* in a cup, let alone anything else.

Father John didn't answer. Standing up, he walked a little unsteadily to the bar and came back with something in a strange-shaped glass. Yellow, red, and orange liquid swirled together in it, and a skewer with fruit had been stuck in alongside a tiny, brightly colored paper umbrella far smaller than I'd imagined. A fact for which I was grateful.

"I do not understand. Was what I am drinking not a drink?" I frowned.

"Alcohol, Cass. Alcohol."

"Oh." I accepted the drink and smelled it. He'd had me try some of his beer once, and I'd hated it. This, on the other hand, smelled like sweetness and fruit. I tried a little and smiled. "This is good. But I do not understand the umbrella."

"'S a garnish, child. Just t'make the drink look pretty."

I pulled the umbrella out and fumbled with it until it closed. I then lay it on the table before I took a sip. I couldn't identify the kinds of fruit in the drink, but I enjoyed it. "Much better than beer."

Father John chuckled. "If you say so. *Sláinte*." He took a swallow of his beer. "Mary Beth is back in the shelter again. Left her father's house 'cause he skipped town again without tellin' her." His words slurred a little.

I grunted, shaking my head and sighing. "Someone should have a talk with that man. He cannot keep walking away from his daughter like that. It is wrong."

"I've been tryin', but he ain't listenin'. She's seventeen, so there's no laws against it, but..." He trailed off. His accent—Irish, I'd learned—was always thicker when he drank. "Reminds me of my Betsy. She were a good girl when we were kids."

"Betsy? You had a wife?"

"No, no. My sister. Died years ago."

"I am sorry. I did not know." The words felt a little empty, but I didn't know what else to say in the face of his grief.

"Aye, 'twas a hell of a thing. I saw it. Don't know how it got in the house, but there it was. All fire and darkness like they describe 'em in the Bible."

My frown deepened, but I just let him talk, not sure where he was going with this, though something in the pit of my stomach suggested it was nowhere good. I sipped my drink, understanding why he'd said I needed one. Alcohol seemed to have no effect on me no matter how much I imbibed, however. We'd tested it once out of curiosity.

Father John stared down at the table like he'd forgotten his beer. "What I'm sayin' is if... if that *thing* exists, maybe what you're sayin' about what you are ain't so farfetched."

The weight of what he said seemed lost on him, but I nodded. "True evil exists, father. I have seen it and faced it. And I have fallen to it. But true goodness also exists. 'The Lord is good, a stronghold in the day of trouble; he knows those who take refuge in Him.'"

"Not many can quote the book of Nahum, Cassiel." Father John chuckled.

"It is not a book that brings much peace. It is a warning against those who ignore Him." I took a swallow of my drink. "I find it a comfort to know that, whatever happens, He will not ignore evil in the world. Nor shall I." My mind wandered back to poor Mary Beth, but I didn't know what to do about it. Her father, after all, had made his choices.

"Where were you, then?" He lifted his head and stared at me. "Where were you when it took 'em? My sister, her husband, the boy. Where were you?" He enunciated the words like stones and cast them at me.

I reeled back like he'd struck me. "Father, I—"

"What good are angels if they stand by while demons slaughter the innocent?" He slapped his hand on the table, and beer sloshed over the rim of his glass.

My brows furrowed. I had no answers for him, and my hurt must have shown on my face because Father John looked away shortly thereafter, his eyes wet and breath shaking.

Silence hung thick and heavy between us for a long time, and I tried to come up with the words to say to him. I hadn't been there because I had been at my post, guarding one of the gates of Heaven, but his anger wasn't unjustified. And beyond that anger, the pain he felt—and the fear—spoke more to me than the angry words he spat. They cut deeper.

What good are angels?

Despite knowing the logical answer, I had seen so much suffering and anger among those here that it was a question I had no way to respond to. What good *was* I? I lowered my head. The only thing I could think to say was, "I am here now."

He didn't answer for what felt like ages, but when he did, his voice was more even. "That you are." Father John lifted his glass and drained it. "Finish your drink. I think it's time to go home."

I did so, though drinking it all at once like I did made my head ache from the cold. I then picked up the little paper umbrella and pocketed it. I couldn't tell you why I did it, but maybe some part of me wanted to remember this moment and this conversation.

I stood up and supported Father John, who was less steady on his feet. We paid at the bar and then left, heading out onto the street. I half-carried him most of the way home, allowing him to use my strength to keep himself upright as he teetered. When we reached the rectory, I held Father John up while he fumbled with his keys and unlocked the door.

Inside, I carried him up to his bed and laid him out on it despite his protests. I then removed his shoes and covered him with the blankets. "Sleep, father."

He mumbled something I didn't understand and closed his eyes. I sat with him for a few minutes, praying for peace and protection before I rose and left the house, turning off the lights and locking the door behind me.

The cool night air carried the promise of rain. Rather than head inside and go to bed to lie awake for hours, I stuck my hands in my pockets and walked. My fingers touched the little umbrella, and I gently rolled it between them as I wandered the church grounds, trying to think of an adequate answer to his question.

What good are angels?

CHAPTER 6

The next morning, I rose and stretched, exhausted after my late-night wanderings. Unlike most residents of the church, I had my own space, insomuch as it was. My room was a janitor's closet we'd cleared out. It contained a camp cot with a thick foam pad on it as well as a set of shelves for the few personal effects I owned. All I had to my name was a copy of the Bible, that bright red-and-yellow cocktail umbrella, some clothing, a battered old wallet, and a ring of keys to the church buildings.

A small nightlight glowed in one corner of the room, offering the only illumination in the room. Of course, I use the term "room" loosely. It was about seven feet deep and six feet wide, designed for mop and bucket storage, not people. Father John had been very clear that I was not to tell anyone he let me sleep in there since it was against something he called "fire codes", whatever that meant. I didn't mind. Having any space at all of my own was a blessing since, after an eternity of silence and nigh-complete isolation, I found constant interaction overwhelming.

During my first few weeks staying here, I had been almost unable to function when there were more than one or two other people present, and even after nearly a year on the ground, I still found it difficult to manage around others. Father John must have recognized that, which was why he'd retrofitted this room to suit my humble needs.

The clothes I owned were all secondhand from the donations bin and didn't fit extremely well. I had to wear a canvas belt with my pants to prevent them from sagging off my hips, and the t-shirts were a little tight on me through the shoulders. I made do since I didn't have much else for options and was grateful to have anything to wear after having experienced the chill of Boston winter.

I dressed and stepped out of the cramped space, locking the door behind me. My room opened into a hallway on the second floor of the building near the meeting rooms and elevator. As was my usual morning routine, I left the church proper after brushing my teeth and washing up in one of the bathrooms and headed into the shelter to help Dust in the kitchen. We always fed the people who spent the night at the shelter a good breakfast before they left and went out into the city, and I often made sandwiches to take out to those who had no food for lunch.

It was, I learned, an unusual approach to such a thing since most just provided a bed to sleep in for a few hours before turning everyone out terribly early in the morning and not allowing them back into the building until quite late. Father John had different beliefs about how to handle the local homeless population, and he had spoken to me quite passionately on the matter more than once. He quoted Matthew 25:40 often and took that injunction ("whatever you did for the least of these brothers of Mine you did for Me") as a significant portion of his calling to ministry.

Whatever else might be said about Father John, he walked the path of his calling with his whole heart and did his best to tend to the community with everything he had. I respected those qualities in him and found myself feeling blessed every time I learned of one of his new projects to try and provide some stability for the city.

His most recent project, some community park cleanup effort, was garnering some push back from people in the area, or so he'd confided in me one night after several beers. He felt strongly that making the park across the street from the church a safer, cleaner place would benefit everyone. Also, trying to discourage drug sales in the area would protect the children who lived in the projects in the area immediately around us, including the homeless who spent most of their time there.

The kitchen in the shelter was a large room with stainless steel fixtures that we kept so clean, they gleamed. Dust was a tough taskmaster and treated the place like he treated the professional kitchens he worked in. While it was, at times, frustrating to be growled at like he tended to, I knew he was a good man; he worked hard and donated his time and expertise to the people here without asking for anything in return. Sometimes, he even provided ingredients out of his own money when the kitchen came in over budget or during holidays.

Dust was already there when I arrived, and he pressed a cup of hot coffee into my hands made the way I had learned to enjoy it: a lot of cream and sugar. It did nothing to wake me up, but drinking it was a communal act, and I enjoyed the taste and warmth. He then shot me a smile, his tusks gleaming in the overhead lights. "First one here," he said.

"Good morning, Dust," I said and took a sip of my coffee. "How are you this morning?" How he was so lively after just waking up, I'll never know, but it seemed to me he sprang out of bed to start each morning with more energy than most people had all day.

"Every morning I'm on my feet is a good 'un." He turned his back to me, already starting to prepare the first batch of eggs. He'd cracked a number of them into a steel bowl on the counter. At that point in my life, everything I knew about cooking came from Dust, although what I knew wasn't much. I could scramble eggs, prepare sandwiches, and slice vegetables well enough, but anything much more complex remained out of my grasp.

I downed my coffee and threw away the paper cup it had been in before washing my hands thoroughly. I then approached him. "I can do the eggs if you would like to do something else."

"One of these days, I'm gonna have to teach you to cook sausages."

"The last time I tried, the fire alarm went off and upset everybody."

"A little fire in the kitchen doesn't mean you should stop trying." He pointed one large, green finger in my direction. "Gotta keep at it or you won't learn." Then he relinquished the bowl of eggs and moved across the kitchen to start something else.

I took his place and got to work. We didn't talk much after that, too focused on our preparations. Breakfast was typically a simple affair with eggs, toast, cereal, and usually some kind of meat. Most mornings, it was just Dust and me in the kitchen that early—

the other volunteers typically worked evening shifts. There were a number of them I'd grown to know, but none so regular or skilled as Dust.

I prepared the eggs as he'd taught me, scrambling them on the flat cooktop and dumping them into the steam table tray. Once it was full, I took it out to the table and set it into its position. By then, people were milling about the dining area, and I got sleepy smiles from those who recognized me.

Early on, I had been rather vocal about my nature as an angel, which had earned me a reputation for being "a little off" among those here. I doubted any of them believed I was what I said I was, but most of them were kindly indulgent of my apparent delusion. I learned, over time, to keep my nature to myself, though by then, I had already become known as "The Angel of St. Mary's" to some of the regulars. I couldn't quite tell if they meant it as a joke or sincerely, and I'd never really wanted to ask in case it was a mockery.

I smiled to them and headed back into the kitchen to make more eggs—they went fast in the mornings—and passed Dust carrying a tray of sausages. He plucked one off it and shoved it in my mouth. "You gotta eat, too," he grumbled as he went by. I didn't argue and ate it on my way back to the griddle.

The next hour or so more or less passed the same way with me refilling the eggs or pulling cartons of milk out of the refrigerator to put out front until everyone was sated. I spotted Mary Beth sitting alone at one of the tables and frowned, but with the kitchen crew being just the two of us, I didn't have time to try and speak to her before we finished breakfast service. And by then, she was gone.

I hadn't spoken to her much, but the few times I had, she'd been soft-spoken and sweet. How somebody could just abandon her for weeks on end sometimes, I didn't know, and thinking about it too long made my chest ache with a combination of anger and sadness.

After everyone else was fed and the dishes were done, I made myself two scrambled eggs and set them aside before cleaning the griddle and turning it off. When I turned back to my plate, there were a couple pieces of toast, several sausages, and a boxed portion of orange juice sitting next to it. Dust was nowhere to be seen, but I had no question he was responsible for it.

I prayed over the meal and ate alone in the kitchen before washing up my dishes and headed into the sanctuary. Father John was usually in his office about that time, and I wanted to talk to him about our conversation the night before. The question he'd asked had haunted me all night and made it difficult to sleep.

As I always did, I paused in the sanctuary and enjoyed the sight of the morning sun pouring through the stained-glass windows of the sanctuary. For all the world had very little understanding of the divine much of the time, the decision to build churches as they did hinted at the Father's involvement in their lives, even if only a little.

I smiled and drew in a deep breath through my nose, expecting the scent of incense and wood polish as usual. Instead, I smelled copper and brimstone.

CHAPTER 7

I knew those scents. Everything felt like it was moving too slowly as I rushed toward Father John's office on the far side of the sanctuary and flung open his door, having drawn as much of my meager remaining Grace into me as I could, but I knew the instant I saw him, it was too late.

Father John sat in his chair, leaned back with his mouth open in a silent scream and eyes rolled back into his head. Blood covered him and the floor so thickly that the carpet squished when I moved toward him. While I hadn't seen who or what was responsible, I felt the taint of demonic influence so thick in the air, it was almost a pressure on my skin.

"Father John!" I reached out for him, touching his shoulder.

Despite knowing it was too late, I tried nonetheless to heal him. I hadn't tried to use my Grace since I'd fallen, and I had no idea what remained. My heart beat so hard it hurt, and my vision faded to pinpoints of light as I threw every part of me into trying to heal him.

A sound distracted me: a woman's scream. I stumbled back from Father John and looked toward the sound, seeing the elderly church secretary in the doorway. She wore a skirt that hung down to her hooves and a bright, sunny yellow cardigan. Her short horns curled back into her poofy hairdo, almost hiding them if you didn't know they were there. Mrs. Callas, a satyr, was one of the church's most beloved members. She had worked as Father John's assistant and as church secretary for as long as any of them could remember. While she didn't much like me, she was a kind woman in general who worked hard for the parish and who supported Father John's various projects.

Mrs. Callas looked like she was about to faint, so I tore myself away from Father John and moved toward her. She stumbled back and away from me, throwing a gnarled hand out as though to defend herself. "How could you!" Her voice came out breathless and high pitched. "After he took you in like he did. How could you do this to him?"

I opened my mouth to answer, but nothing came out. How could she think I had done this? I was no demon and didn't have the power to accomplish such an act. I didn't have time to answer before she had her phone out of her pocket and was calling someone while rushing away from me as quickly as her hooves could take her.

It occurred to me to follow her. To clear my name. Instead, I sat down on one of the pews as a peculiar sort of numbness overtook me, crawling up my body from my feet until all of me felt like television static. The world felt so far away and so empty. Like nothing this morning had been real. I could still taste eggs and sausage and orange juice, but the memory of eating in the kitchen seemed distant now. Like it had happened years ago.

My chest tightened, and I struggled for air. The copper scent came with each breath, so thick I could almost taste it, and my head spun. After so long as a gate guardian, blood and war had ceased to shock me, but never before had someone I'd known, someone I'd cared for...

Unable to do anything else, I dropped onto the kneeler and clasped my hands. I didn't have the words. My soul cried out in a wordless scream of anguish, confusion, and fury. So many people think prayer is words. What I did in that moment had no structure. No language could have expressed the silent thunder in my heart. But make no mistake—every tear sliding down my face, every tremble of my body, every gasping breath were all prayer.

I don't know how long I stayed there, but police officers flooded the building. Their weapons were drawn and pointed at me, and a chorus of voices told me to get on the ground and put my hands behind my head. Father John had told me once that I was to obey these men called police, that they had authority and power, that to do otherwise would not end well for me since I was homeless and strange. Out of that learning, I lifted my hands and followed their instructions, collapsing to the floor and lacing my sticky fingers behind my head, vaguely aware that half-dry blood was now rubbing into my hair.

They put handcuffs on me and yanked me up. Were I not as strong as I am, it could have injured me with how rough they were, but I didn't struggle or argue. Instead, I lowered my head and shuffled along with them as they took me out of the church and into the bright morning sun.

I suspect the chaos and sirens must have attracted them, but people thronged the sidewalk, pressing in to stare at the spectacle of the police walking me out of the church and bundling me into the back seat of one of their cars. They didn't ask me anything or even really address me while they did so, and I didn't volunteer anything to them. After all, what could I say? They would never believe a demon had killed Father John.

When we arrived at the police station, they pulled me out of the back seat and marched me inside through a side door. They sat me down in a barren room with some sort of writing scribed all over it. I couldn't read any of it, since it wasn't written in English or Enochian, so I couldn't even guess at its purpose. After getting my name, they sat me down in a chair and cuffed my hands to a ring on the table in front of me. They then left the room.

I didn't know what to expect and just sat there, staring at my hollow-eyed reflection in the glass across from me. While I felt confident I could have torn the cuffs off if I needed to, I didn't want to provoke them by making them feel as though I were a threat. After all, I wasn't one, and I hadn't done what I had been accused of.

After a long wait, a tall, thin Black man entered the room and sat across from me, his lips pressed into a thin line. After introducing himself as Detective Greene and giving me a long spiel about what I could and could not say, he finally asked, "So what happened?"

I took a deep breath and closed my eyes. "I smelled blood when I walked into the sanctuary after helping with breakfast at the shelter. I was worried for Father John, so I ran into his office. Which is when I found him like…" I couldn't make myself say it.

"You two didn't get into a fight or anything? He didn't make you angry?"

My brows lowered. "He upset me last night, but we did not argue. He had been drinking, so I took him home and put him to bed before going for a walk." He'd told me not to talk about the closet, so I left that out.

The man wrote something in a notebook. "What did he say that upset you?"

"It is complicated. I do not see how that is related—"

"Answer the question, sir."

I didn't see a need to correct him. "He was angry that his sister had died years ago. And he was asking me what good was I that I was not there to help."

More writing. "Did you know him then?"

I shook my head. "No. I have only known him for a year. I do not know when his sister died, but it was before we met."

"Then why did he blame you?"

"Because I am an angel, and his sister was killed by a demon, and he wanted to know what good angels are if they cannot protect people from demons." I knew telling the truth was a mistake the moment I said it, but I had nothing else to offer. How else could I explain it?

That made him pause and look up at me, his brows furrowing. "Angels? Demons? What is this, a television show?"

The notion offended me, and I had to take a deep, slow breath to avoid snapping at him. My emotions felt raw and frayed, and the numbness was beginning to fade, replaced with anger. "No. I am telling you the truth. You asked me."

"Did you see this supposed demon?" His eyes narrowed a little, and he shook his head. This time his note-taking seemed reluctant.

"No, but I sensed its presence."

"Uh-huh. We're gonna have a mage come in and check you for dark magic residue. And we're going to get your fingerprints and a DNA sample if you consent."

I had no idea what most of that meant, so I just nodded. If it meant clearing my name, I'd do just about anything they asked.

Though no matter what I said, I couldn't get them to take my warnings about the demon seriously.

After what felt like an eternity of them getting prints off my fingers, collecting saliva from my mouth, taking my photo, and having another officer come in and do some sort of magical investigation, they removed the cuffs and let me go after telling me not to leave town and saying they'd probably want to talk to me again.

They then walked me out of the police station and left me on the sidewalk out front. I stood still, staring at my feet for a long time before I lifted my head and looked around, realizing I had absolutely no idea where I was. Other than my time in Massachusetts General Hospital, I had not left the few blocks right around the church except to drink with Father John. At least I remembered what he'd told me about the T and what stop the church was near.

Frowning, I looked down at my hands, still black with ink from the fingerprinting. Rusty lines lay under my fingernails. My vision swam a little as I realized what it was. *Father, I don't know what to do next.* I didn't want to go home, but at the same time, I had no idea where else in the world to go. And people there relied on me. Dust and Jim and Eirlas would need my help tomorrow just as they had today.

But, somehow, I couldn't imagine tomorrow. A world without Father John in it—even if I knew where he was and that he was safe and in the arms of our true Father—didn't feel like one I wanted to stay in.

CHAPTER 8

I arrived back at the church at mid-afternoon and stood outside for a while, just staring at the sanctuary. If a demon had been able to enter the church at all, it must have been a powerful one. Faith could keep many demons at bay. A lesser one couldn't enter a sanctuary without bursting into flames, which meant that whatever had come for Father John had to be either an archdemon or one of their top servants.

While there were demons of many types and powers, archdemons were the ones I worried about the most. Archdemons were those who had once been angels—like Lucifer. Like I could be if I chose to walk that road. I trembled and shook my head. If we had an archdemon in the city, I had to do something. I just didn't know what.

Before I fell, my post had been at one of the gates of Heaven. I'd spent eternity there, watching, waiting, and alone. Unlike some of my siblings who came and went to Earth and interacted with its inhabitants, I had seen only the spirits of those carried to Heaven by the other angels.

I sighed, chewing on my lip. Hunting down a demon in the mortal world would have proven child's play for many of my siblings, but I hadn't the faintest idea of how to accomplish a thing like that. And with the police—the only force I knew of who could help such an effort—unwilling or unable to assist me, that left me at a dead end.

"You doing all right?"

The voice startled me, and I spun toward it, muscles tense, ready to defend myself. But I relaxed when I recognized who it was.

Jim held up his hands in a placating motion. "Easy there. It's just me." He rolled his wheelchair a little closer, having stayed out of range before addressing me. Jim worked with a lot of veterans and people with PTSD, so he was always careful on his approach. He'd talked to me about it once or twice when I'd helped him set up for some of his meetings. "I heard about…" Jim trailed off and looked down, his shoulders slumping a little. "I heard."

I swallowed hard and nodded. "Yes. Father John is dead." I didn't know what else to say about it beyond, "I did not do it."

When I qualified that, Jim frowned, shaking his head. "I wouldn't have thought you'd do such a thing, Cassiel. Which is exactly what I told the police when they asked me about it." He came up beside me and faced the church. "It's hard to believe he's gone. I was just talking to him yesterday about some plans I had for a second veterans' group meeting during the week."

"I do not know what we are going to do. What usually happens in situations like this?"

"The bishop will send a temporary replacement until someone permanent is found. And we'll have to put together a funeral. Usually, that'd be the family's job, but… Father John didn't have anyone but his sister. And she died years ago."

The reminder of our last conversation threatened to choke me. "How does one plan a funeral?" I looked at the ground, following the cracks in the pavement as though I could find answers there.

"Don't worry about it. You, me, Dust, Eirlas, and Mrs. Callas will figure it out." Jim patted my arm.

"I do not think Mrs. Callas will want me to help. It is probably better if I do not try." The image of her scrambling back away from me, her eyes wide with fear and whole body trembling flooded my mind, and I shut my eyes to try and block it out.

Jim sighed. "She'll come around."

I put my hands in my pockets as they began to tremble. "I did not kill him. I would not have. I could not have done it like that even if I tried. It is not something even possible for me. I tried to tell her that, but she would not listen."

"Come with me. You should probably sit down for a little while." He headed down the sidewalk past the Sunday school building and over toward the small playground we had at the end of the complex without waiting for me to answer. I followed, knowing an order when I heard one.

For all the sanctuary itself was not particularly big given that it had been built in the 1800s, the church's outbuildings (including the rectory) took up an entire city block on Westview St. across from Harambee Park. Most of the adjacent buildings were industrial or office buildings, which made it an odd place for a church, but I'd never really asked about its history much, though I knew it predated everything else in the vicinity.

Jim led me into the playground, and I sunk down on one of the structures, resting my elbows on my knees with my eyes downcast. The bright vinyl paint covering the playground equipment felt at odds with the heaviness of my spirit, and I considered that in silence for a time. Of all the people at the church, other than Father John, Jim was the one I felt most understood around. I hadn't talked to him about what I was beyond our initial introduction, but he had accepted that I was a stranger in a strange land and didn't mind my awkward ways. He also knew the value of quiet presence and just sat nearby while I tried to scrape my thoughts together.

I told him what had happened, what I'd seen, what I recognized. I tried to stop that last part since I knew he wouldn't believe me, but some part of me had to tell him the whole story. To his credit, Jim just listened while I spoke and said nothing. When I'd finished, I wiped my face with my shirt and jumped a little when Jim touched my leg. He didn't move his hand. "Cass, how do you recognize demons?"

I swallowed hard. "I have dealt with them before. And I mean actual demons, Jim, not theoretical or hyperbole."

"I know what you meant." He squeezed my knee, the contact and pressure reassuring. "If you're right, and this is something that dark, we'll need to tell the bishop."

"Why?" I laughed bitterly. "They will not believe me. Nobody does."

"I do."

I lifted my head in a sharp motion and looked at him. "You... actually believe me?"

Jim nodded. "I've seen enough things in this world to know better than to discount it." He sat back and looked upward maybe at the sky or the steeple—I couldn't tell which. "I'll tell you about it sometime. But right now isn't the time."

"How much do you know about demons?"

"Not much. I know they're tempters or parts of the armies of Hell or things like that. Just what I've read in the Bible, which doesn't do a deep dive on the subject. Or at least the main body doesn't, anyway. I know there's more in the Book of Enoch, but the Apocrypha have never really spoken to me."

"In order for a demon to have entered the church and attack Father John in his office, it would have needed to walk through the sanctuary."

Jim scowled. "Isn't hallowed ground supposed to keep them out?"

I nodded. "Yes. Which means this is not a lesser demon. This has to be an archdemon. If that is the case, and I am right, this is the beginning of something bad, and there will be more deaths." I ran my fingers through my short hair and gripped into it near the back of my head. Father John had helped me cut it. He said the short, rather masculine cut suited me, and it was easy to care for. The fact that he wouldn't be there to help me cut it again struck me as a sudden pang, and tears stung my eyes all over again.

"An archdemon? Is that like an archangel?"

Jim's question drew me back to the present, and I cleared my throat, lifting my head. "Yes. They are the most powerful forces Hell has on the field."

"Why would one of those be *here*, and why would it attack Father John?"

I sighed. "I do not know. It could have to do with me and what I am, but—"

"What you are?"

I shook my head. Even if he believed me when I told him about the demon, there was no guarantee, and I didn't want to make him question me now. Particularly when there was so much on the line. "I do not talk about it."

"Maybe it's time you did."

"You will not believe me. You did not before."

"Try me."

I stood up and sighed, glancing around. There were people here and there, but none were paying attention, and I had come to realize that, generally, people see very little. They are focused on their own worlds, their own spaces, and don't tend to look beyond that unless coaxed. It was a risk, but if I was going to hunt an archdemon, I'd need whatever help I could get.

I chewed my lip a moment before summoning my wings. All six of them. Father John had seen them once, and after that, he had made sure to acquire clothing designed for winged beings and never once commented on their number. Many creatures had wings, so it wasn't difficult to fish used pieces out of the donations bin. Mine had strips of Velcro since I didn't have wings all the time, so it made a rather loud tearing sound when they appeared and pushed the slits in my shirt open.

My feathers are a soft, ashen gray color and quite broad in scope. My primary wings, the middle set, connect to my body around my shoulder blades. Revelation describes us as covering our faces and feet with the other sets of wings, and while that is possible, it is a mistake to think they are on our heads and feet. My upper wings are less than half the size of my primaries and rest at the base of my neck where it joins my shoulders, though if I stretch, I can reach them around my eyes. The bottom ones are a little over half the size of my primaries, and their span is a little longer than I am tall, and they attach to my back down near where my spine joins my pelvis.

Angel wings come in many colors and shapes, and mine had been built for long-distance flight or gliding rather than swift or silent flight. I hadn't used them since my fall and rarely used them before, but I knew what they could do just as I knew I could handle any weapon I put my hand to. I had been built with that understanding imprinted into me.

Whether it was the sound or the wings, Jim jumped and stared for a second before averting his eyes. He didn't say anything for so long, I started to think I had done something to offend him. When he finally did speak, his voice was hushed and almost reverent. "I didn't…"

"I do not talk about it anymore. Father John said I should not, and I learned that few believe." I banished my wings and set about putting my shirt to rights. "Should I have said, 'Be not afraid?'" I was half-joking as I said it, knowing many of the host said such things before revealing themselves because creatures of the Earth often don't respond well to celestial beings. But Jim's unwillingness to look at me set me on edge, and I started to worry I'd made a mistake.

Jim shook his head. "No, no. I just… hadn't expected to see one of you *here*. And we're not really meant to look on celestials directly. Couldn't you strike me blind or something?"

I laughed for what felt like the first time in an eternity. "Perhaps if I were not fallen. But you have not gone blind yet, and you have been talking to me for months."

"I suppose that's true." Jim lifted his gaze, though his expression remained cautious. "You said you're fallen. What does that mean, exactly? I know it's mentioned in the Bible, but… you don't strike me as a demon or a rebel."

I swallowed hard, not relishing the question. "It means I disobeyed the Father and was cast out. I am unwanted."

"Isn't He supposed to be forgiving and compassionate? God is love, after all."

"It works differently for you down here than it does for celestial beings." I didn't really want to explain how Heaven worked, and I wasn't sure I could anyway. Or should. It wasn't a mystery that should be known to those in the world, and it wasn't my place to change that. I had already defied the Father's will once, and I didn't think it prudent to continue to push my boundaries.

Jim nodded. Neither of us spoke for a while, but the silence was a little less comfortable than it had been. I could see Jim's questions on his face before he blurted out the question I'd been avoiding since my fall. "So what happened?"

CHAPTER 9

Father John had asked me that question once, and I'd avoided it. He'd never broached the subject again, maybe because he'd not really believed or, if he did, he didn't want to know. Not really. Then again, he could have just been trying to respect my privacy. Now I would never know for certain.

Jim watched me expectantly, his expression wary. I didn't blame him for it. After what had just happened, and what had done it, I wouldn't have been very trusting, either.

But that didn't make it any easier.

"I... really do not like talking about it, Jim," I said after a long while. "But if you really want to know, I will tell you." I rubbed the scars that stretched from my jaw down to my chest, a perfect set of four. The edges were drawn from where they'd been stitched, though the stitches themselves hadn't scarred. Just the wounds. They ached as if to remind me of my failures. Of my foolishness. Like I could have forgotten.

Jim sighed. "Normally, I wouldn't press, Cass, but under the circumstances..."

"I understand. For all you know, I could be on the side of the demon in question. You do not trust me." Saying it out loud hurt, even if I understood it.

He shook his head, leaning his elbows on the arms of his wheelchair. "I'm a pretty good judge of character, Cass. I trust you. If I thought you were trouble, or evil, I would've spoken up to Father John ages ago. I'm asking because if what you are, *who* you are, has anything to do with what happened, I can't be walking into this blind."

I wasn't sure he was telling me the whole truth, but I saw no point in arguing. Even if he did trust me, he had a point. I wasn't sure if this demon had anything to do with me or not, but if it did, it wouldn't be fair to send Jim in unprepared. If I'd convinced Father John to believe me, maybe none of this would've happened in the first place.

None of that made this easier.

I took a slow, deep breath and leaned back against the playground equipment I sat on, one of my legs bouncing a little with unspent energy as I tried to decide how far back to go. How much to tell him. I supposed I could gloss over the details and try to frame it in a way a mortal would understand.

"My full name is Cassiel."

"The archangel?"

"No. That is a mistake in your transcription. I am a seraph, but I am not an archangel. Your texts say we guard the throne of Heaven, and that is true. But more than that, we are also guardians of the gates of Heaven against incursions from Hell."

"So... that makes you powerful, right?"

I sighed. "I was, yes. My life's purpose was to guard a specific gate into Heaven. It wasn't used often, and I spent most of my time alone. So, my abilities tend toward combat and war. Tactics, things like that." I waved a hand.

"For how long?"

I blinked. "How long have I been a seraph?" The question confused me, and I frowned at him.

Jim shook his head. "How long were you alone?"

"I do not know how to explain it to you in terms you would understand."

"So... a long time?"

"I have been alive since the beginning, Jim. Time is strange to me. And until I fell, I did not mark days as you do since day and night are not really relevant for where I was stationed."

He nodded and made a gesture as though to encourage me to continue. "Sorry to interrupt."

I chewed the inside of my lip while weighing how much to say. "Over the eons I was stationed there, a demon visited me on occasion. He called himself Arazael. For a long time, I did nothing but send him away and threaten him, but he persisted, claiming he just wanted to talk.

"In my loneliness and foolishness, I gave in. I rarely saw anyone, and it was because of his presence that I realized I was, in fact, lonely. That I wanted companionship. Needed it, even. And since I had no one else, over time, I grew to accept Arazael's company." I sighed, shaking my head at my own idiocy. It hurt to think about. Even after a year, the events preceding my fall felt fresh in my mind and heart, and the ache from them hadn't diminished.

"Why didn't you just kill him the first time?"

"I was not supposed to leave my post, and he knew it, so he stayed just far enough away that if I were to attempt to pursue, I would be abandoning the gate. So I could not have. Which gave him the opportunity to talk. I know it was foolish, but..." I trailed off.

Jim tilted his head. "I never thought about it that way. That an angel could be lonely, I mean. I suppose I thought you are all just... one in the spirit."

"We are. I was. But that does not mean standing alone at a gate for eternity and not seeing another for decades on end is not lonely if you come to understand and realize companionship. Over time, Arazael and I became sort of friends. I did not trust him, of course, but he came frequently and would tell me things of the world or talk to me about nothing or anything. But I listened. We shared jokes and laughter.

"At the end, I came to believe he may be repentant and had begun to consider that he could be, perhaps, redeemed." My throat tightened a little, and I had to pause to compose myself before telling the end of my story. "The day I fell, he came to me, wild-eyed, bleeding, and afraid. He said he had defected from Hell and that there was an army after him. He begged me for help, saying they would kill him. I did not want that to happen, so I allowed him close. When the other demons came into view, I stepped away from the gate to engage them. To protect Arazael." My hands shook, and I looked down at them. "The next thing I knew, Arazael's claws were in my neck, and he had run past me into Heaven. The other demons descended on me, but they were hardly a challenge. I had, however, failed my duty. I had allowed a demon into Heaven.

"When I was called to account for my actions, I learned Arazael had died almost immediately after passing me, so the results were not catastrophic. But that did not prevent me from needing to atone for it. When the others learned I had been fooled, swayed, I was cast down. Which was when I met Father John." I rubbed at the scars on my neck, and Jim's gaze followed my motion.

"Just like that? No opportunity for forgiveness?"

"I was sent here, not to Hell. So I suppose that is chance enough." I shrugged, trying to stop my leg from bouncing. Arazael's death still hurt. Even if he had been lying, even if he had been a weasel, even if he had been using me, it still hurt. And I had lain awake many nights wondering if it were possible for a demon to be redeemed and if some part of him had been genuine. Perhaps it was foolish of me to consider it, but I had always believed that repentance was not conditional, and if even a demon sought redemption—truly sought it—they could perhaps find their way. But who was I to question such things after what happened?

Jim crossed his arms, his expression thoughtful. "Thank you for telling me. I'm sorry for what happened to you."

"It was my own fault. Do not pity me."

"Maybe, but that doesn't make it hurt any less. I can't imagine being alone that long. It's no wonder you were lonely and no surprise you were prey for something like that. Reminds me of the elderly folk here who are taken advantage of. It happens. It's just how people are."

"I am not people."

"Aren't you?" Jim tilted his head and poked at me a few times. "Sure look like people to me. And even if you weren't before, you are now. So could this Arazael have survived?"

I shook my head. "I deeply doubt it. The angelic host would have smote him on the spot once he passed me."

"Then why would he even try to get in? That seems just suicidal. Pointless."

I shrugged and sighed. That was a question I'd asked myself over and over again with no answers. "I do not know."

Jim looked toward the sanctuary, changing the subject. "If only an archdemon could get in there and cause that kind of havoc, could kill a holy man on consecrated ground, what can we do about it?"

"If I can find the thing, I may be able to destroy it."

"I thought you lost your power?"

"Most of it but not all." I conjured a tiny flicker of holy fire to my fingertips. Holy fire looked much like regular flame but brighter and pure white. It wasn't even really flame—it didn't move or look exactly like fire, but it was close enough that the earthbound had called it "holy fire." In truth, it defies the way most creatures understand the world to work, so describing it is difficult using the mortal tongue. The correct name for it is in Enochian, which doesn't translate well to English.

Jim squinted against the bright light and didn't look directly at it. I doused the flame to avoid both attention and causing Jim discomfort. "That is what blinds people who look at it too long," I explained.

"Why didn't you warn me?" Jim threw his hands up.

"That amount could not have done such a thing unless you stared at it for a long time." I shook my head and stood. I felt weak and dizzy all at once and frowned, having to grab onto the frame of the jungle gym above my head.

When I wavered, Jim scowled. "All right, we need to get you inside. When was the last time you ate anything or had anything to drink?"

"This morning. I was with the police for a long time."

"All right. Let's get you fed, then we'll figure out our next steps." He had me push him inside, claiming he was tired, but I was pretty sure it was a ploy to make sure I didn't fall over since, if I were holding the handles of the wheelchair, I had something to lean on. As lies went, it was a pretty weak one since Jim was a very strong, fit man from using his upper body to propel himself in his chair. And he certainly didn't look tired. Nonetheless, I was grateful for his attempt to spare my dignity.

CHAPTER 10

I remember little of the next few days as we prepared for Father John's funeral, but I was just one in a sea of many. For all St. Mary's was a rather small church in physical size, its impact on the community was significant, and everyone played a role in the preparations. I mostly moved things—picking them up and putting them down, as Dust called it—and tried not to think too much. If I stopped to mull over what had happened, the grief overwhelmed me, so I counteracted it with motion. I cleaned the entire complex spotless, scrubbing every corner of every room until it shone when I wasn't helping people move furniture around or listening to members of staff work on their eulogies.

I hadn't been invited to speak, which was something I didn't mind so much. Dust and Jim were offended that I wasn't being given the opportunity, but I didn't believe I could have said much of anything anyway. I have never been much of an orator.

I met the new priest, Father Arthur Demoyne, on the day of the funeral when he addressed everyone who worked in the shelter. He gathered the staff together in one of the various meeting rooms the minute the funeral was over and informed us that changes were going to be made. With all due respect (a phrase I learned meant "with no respect at all") to Father John's vision, Father Demoyne was cutting the hours of operation and ending the breakfast hours effective immediately.

Dust clenched his fists and let out a low noise before stepping forward. "Look, Father Demoyne, I respect that you're in charge here, but there are a lotta folks who rely on—"

Father Demoyne, who never gave anyone permission to call him Father Arthur, fixed Dust with a narrow-eyed glare as he drew himself up as though he could compete with Dust's height and bulk. Dust came in at about six and a half feet tall and had to weigh over two hundred pounds in muscle and stubbornness. Father Demoyne was somewhat shorter and probably weighed a hundred pounds if caught in his robes in the rain. His elven heritage showed in his ears and slight build, but he didn't have the aching beauty most of them had. Instead, he looked like someone had made his coffee with cottage cheese most of the time. Father Demoyne's wire-framed glasses slid down his long, pointed nose, and he glowered at Dust as though the sheer force of his disapproval could act as a bulwark against the angry orc.

"Father John's extracurricular programs, well intentioned as they were, are not approved by the diocese. He was running them without appropriate backing, and they cannot continue as they were. The shelter and kitchen will remain, but until such a time as—"

"Look, you self-important pinecone," Dust snarled the words down at Father Demoyne, "I fund the breakfast out of my own pocket and do the work. It doesn't cost the church a penny beyond utilities that are already being paid for. It didn't need approval because it wasn't coming out of the budget."

I put a hand on Dust's shoulder to forestall any further argument and opened my mouth to speak, but Jim cut me off. "Father Demoyne, we've just lost a dear friend, and things are uncertain. I'm sure my friend here doesn't intend any disrespect." He shot Dust a withering glare and, for a moment, seemed far larger than he actually was. "Do we, Dust?"

The orc wilted a bit, and his shoulder relaxed a little under my hand. "No."

"I'm sure we can work this out in the coming days, but we'll all have to work together to figure out our new normal." Jim leaned back in his chair, arms crossed. "I'm sorry for the argument, Father Demoyne. We're all just a little overwhelmed with what's happened."

Father Demoyne glared at Dust but relented for now. "Yes, well, of course. Which brings me to my next point." He faced me. "Since you're under police investigation for the murder of Father John, I cannot in good conscience let you continue staying here. You're welcome if you wish to come to me in confession, but many members of the congregation have expressed their discomfort with your presence here."

It felt like all the air had been sucked out of the room, and I couldn't quite draw in a breath. I felt dizzy and sick, but all I could do was nod. Jim and Dust spoke at once to defend me, their voices overlapping. They all sounded so distant.

I jumped so hard, I almost fell when someone touched my arm, and I shook my head, looking toward the contact. "Let's step outside. You don't need to listen to this mess." Eirlas spoke in a quiet voice. He took my arm and drew me out of the room. I stumbled after him, obedient as a lamb, and walked with him down the hall toward the kitchen where he sat me down.

Of the three people who managed the shelter, Eirlas was the one I knew the least. He'd always been kind to me, but we hadn't really talked. I knew only that he was an elf and that he had some kind of history with his family having excommunicated him in the past for some reason or another. At the funeral, I'd learned he had, for a time, struggled with drug addiction, but he seemed to have come through it all right so far as I could tell. He'd spoken about it at the funeral and had credited Father John with his recovery. I couldn't remember the details. Everything had been a blur.

Generally speaking, elves are supernaturally attractive. Of all the races occupying the Earth, the only ones that give them a run for their money in sheer beauty are the fae peoples, to whom they are distantly related. I had seen a few of them here and there, but Eirlas was my primary exposure to elves. Despite the fact that his bone structure was perfectly proportioned, his jaw angular and square, and his cheekbones defined, he always looked a little under-fed to me. Dark circles covered the skin beneath his vibrant green eyes, and he somehow looked thinner than his bone structure should've dictated. I had never talked with him long enough to ask about the cause of any of it, however.

Eirlas pressed a cup of hot coffee into my hands. "Breathe. You look like you're about to faint, Cass." He patted my back with one long-fingered hand. His clear green eyes met mine, and he smiled a little. "Can you do something for me?"

I nodded, focused on trying not to drop my coffee.

"Look around and name five things you see."

The request struck me as odd, but I tried to fight through the fog. "Uh," my voice shook, and I cleared my throat. "The griddle, the ceiling tiles... prep table, walk-in..." I trailed off, looking for a fifth thing while Eirlas stood across the walkway from me, leaning on the aforementioned prep table. "You." My mind felt a little clearer.

"Good. Now, five things you can touch." His tone was patient and quiet, like he was talking to an injured animal.

"Coffee cup, uh... the chair, my clothes, the floor," I stammered, trying to find a fifth. Eirlas reached out, and I took his hand. "You. Again. I guess."

He smiled and squeezed my fingers. His hand felt delicate in mine. If I squeezed, I could've broken every bone in it with no effort at all. "Good job."

"That was a weird question." I shook my head and had some of the coffee, finding the warmth reassuring. Drinking it helped fill the cold, empty place that had formed in my chest during the meeting.

Eirlas nodded. "They're grounding techniques designed to help with panic attacks. A lot of people in the shelter get them, so I've guided people through them a lot." He released my hand and sighed. "Don't worry too much about Father Demoyne. We won't let him kick you out of this place. It's your home, and you're part of our family here. No matter what happens, me, Dust, and Jim have your back. We'll sort something out."

"Why does everyone think I killed him?"

"You were the first one there, and people know you're a little odd, Cass. You don't see things like most people do. It isn't a bad thing, but people who are different get treated like that. You talk about angels and demons and all that, and people just aren't comfortable with it. It scares them. It doesn't even matter if it's true or not."

"You believe me?"

"I believe you didn't kill Father John. I can't claim to understand the rest of it. But as a Christian, I have to believe in angels and demons. They're in the Bible, though I've always understood them to be more theoretical."

Father John had said the same thing, as had several others, and I shook my head, lacking the energy to get into the discussion right now. Besides, this wasn't the place or time. "Thank you, Eirlas."

Dust and Jim burst into the room like a pair of thunderstorms. "Of all the stupid..." Jim growled, his jaw tense and brown eyes so dark, they were nearly black. It took effort to get him angry, and I'd only seen it once before during one of the veterans' groups. Two of the vets had gotten into an argument that had nearly turned physical until Jim barked at them. They'd returned to their seats grumbling but had obeyed him anyway. I didn't know exactly what it meant, but he'd explained he'd been a "drill instructor" for the Marines, which I assumed was more or less a position that involved keeping soldiers in order. Either way, he had a presence to him that tended to make people sit up and take notice when he wanted them to.

"Trying to gut those programs now is an *atrocity*," Dust said. I didn't understand the word, but by context, I knew it wasn't good. "With that new drug on the streets, we need what Father John was doing more than ever. That arrogant, pompous f—"

Eirlas held up his hands to forestall them. "If you're going to bring all that in here, step back outside. I just got Cass calmed down."

Dust scowled and opened his mouth to argue, looked at me, and walked back out of the room. I heard the outside door open and close behind him. Jim, on the other hand, took a slow, deep breath and nodded. "I'm good. I'm good." He rolled over to me and gripped my shoulder. "Until we get this sorted out, you're staying with me. It's not much, but it's a roof."

I put my hand over his and nodded. "All right. Thank you." The numb, panicky feeling started to well up again, but I tried to ignore it.

Eirlas nodded a little. "I can't speak for Dust, but she's welcome with me, too. Between the three of us, we'll make sure she's not on the street."

"I got him to relent and let her keep working in the shelter. Those," Jim clamped his jaw shut for a second before continuing, "*people* in the congregation who are against Cassiel attending have never set foot in this building, and that's not likely to change anytime soon. So she'll be okay to keep helping here."

It felt a little odd to be talked about while I sat between them, but I didn't have the energy to argue. And, in truth, I felt some measure of relief not having to make all these decisions for myself. At least not right now.

Dust walked into the room and went to one of the sinks to wash his hands, and the water came away red. Jim and Eirlas were too busy trying to work out logistics to have noticed, so I stood up and walked over to him. "Are you all right?"

"Yes," Dust grunted. "Just had an argument. With a wall."

"And people say I am the crazy one." I tried to make myself smile, but it felt awkward and out of place.

If Dust noticed, he didn't show it. "You're not crazy, Cass. A little different, but not crazy. Don't let anyone say otherwise." He growled the words. "People are always unkind to things they don't understand."

"That is what Eirlas told me."

"He's right. And he'd know. So'd I. You just keep being who you are. Rest'll sort itself out." He finished washing his hands and dried them with some paper towels that he then kept pressed to his knuckles.

"Jim said I am to stay with him."

"Figured as much. Never seen him this pissed off before. Jim doesn't get pissed."

"Pissed?" I frowned. "Has he urinated on himself?"

That made Dust laugh, and the sound drew everyone's attention. "No. It's a phrase. You know, one of those things? Means he's angry."

"Pissed means urinated. Pissed means angry. Why do words not mean one thing?"

"You know," Dust said, patting my shoulder, "I have no idea."

CHAPTER 11

The four of us parted ways with Jim taking me to collect my few belongings and then out to his dark blue van to drive me to his home. At the time, I didn't know enough to question how he drove without legs, but his van had been configured to allow him to do so. He opened the driver's side back door and slid a ramp out from the bottom of the van, guiding himself up it. The driver's seat faced backwards, toward the cargo area of the van, and I realized it must be on a pivot. Using a couple well-placed handholds, Jim maneuvered himself out of the wheelchair and into the seat, folding the wheelchair and sliding it into a spot designed to hold one. He then hit a button, and the ramp retracted on its own.

One of the first things I'd learned about Jim Hammerson was that he had things more or less under control at all times, and if he needed help, he asked for it. I'd fussed a fair amount when he and I had first met until he sat me down and informed me that he'd been living his life just fine for over a decade before I'd gotten there. He appreciated my desire to help him, but he didn't need it. And if he did, he'd ask. The only time anyone was allowed to touch his chair was when he'd invited it, and I respected him enough to rein myself in. Over the year I'd known him, I'd come to realize he was self-sufficient and more or less like most anyone else at the church, albeit he needed elevators and ramps to get places.

Jim raised an eyebrow in my direction. "You getting in, or...?"

I shook myself and nodded, striding around the front of the van to climb into the passenger's seat. We buckled up, and Jim started the engine, guiding the van out of the parking lot. As we drove through the traditionally awful Boston traffic, neither of us had much to say, both too wrapped up in our thoughts to converse.

I leaned my head on the window beside me and stared out at the road as Jim navigated. I hadn't been in a car more than a few times—Father John had mostly used the T to get places. The Boston Rail Transit System, usually just called the T, is a spidering network of subway tunnels that ties into the commuter rail. I hadn't explored much of it, but Father John had taught me enough to know which stop was home. Had *been* home, I reminded myself.

That came with an unexpected pang. In the space of a week I had lost my friend and now my home. I hadn't been extremely tied to the church, or so I'd thought, until I found myself leaving it. A deep sigh left me, and I closed my eyes, praying for guidance and calm as my thoughts turned toward the task of finding the demon. Despite being certain I was the only one in the situation who had even a ghost of a chance of handling an archdemon, I doubted my capability. I hadn't used my Grace much since my fall, and I didn't know what I could still do or how much power I really had retained.

Of course, if I had to die to destroy the archdemon stalking Boston, I was willing. I'd been created to face them down and prevent them from doing harm to people. But that didn't mean I savored the idea. And, worse, if the demon killed me, and I failed to destroy it, what havoc would it wreak on those I left behind?

Jim put a hand on my knee, and I jumped, opening my eyes and looking at him. "We'll figure this out, Cass. You don't need to fight this alone."

"How did you know what I was thinking?" His perceptiveness never failed to surprise me.

A wry smile crossed his face, and he glanced at me for a second. "It doesn't take a mind reader to know what's in your head. It's the same kinda thing that'd be in anyone's after all this. A lot's happened at once, and none of it was good. I don't blame you for feeling overwhelmed. Beyond that," he grinned at me, "I know how soldiers work. Your brain's already trying to plan your assault with what you think you've got for tools. But you're wrong."

I grunted. "I know well what my capabilities are."

"Sure, of course you do. But you're missing some important data points."

My brows drew together, and I shook my head. "You do not know what this is."

"Cassiel, you are forgetting that you're not fighting this by yourself." He patted my leg firmly before putting his hand back on the wheel. "I get it. You're used to working alone. From what you told me, you've been alone a long, long time. But don't count the rest of us out. Dust and Eirlas? They'll go to the wire to take care of you. You're family."

"I am not related to any of you."

"Not that kind of family. Family can be a lotta things. For some, it's the people they're related to. For others, it's the folks they choose. Eirlas, Dust, and I? We're a family. Brothers. We've been working together a long time and gotten through some rough spots. You're one of us. We'll take care of you."

I fidgeted a little with the ratty hem of the t-shirt I wore. "I did not know they felt so strongly. But... what is coming is more than you can face. You are not equipped to fight demons, Jim. None of you are."

"There are people in the Bible who did it. But even if we can't go toe-to-toe with these bastards, we can back you up."

"Do the others know what I am? Did you tell them?"

Jim shook his head. "That seems like something you should tell them yourself, but... I'd take it slow. I believe you, but it might be harder on them."

"Why *did* you believe me?"

Silence fell between us for a minute, and I didn't press. Spending time with Jim during the various support groups he managed and ran, I'd learned that sometimes waiting and giving someone space to talk was better than asking. Jim was a master of that. He'd just sit quietly, waiting, watching. He could tell when something hurt too much to talk about; he knew when to move away and get coffee; and he knew when to ask questions and how. I admired his ability to do what he called "hold space" and had been trying to learn to do it myself.

"I'll tell you someday, but you aren't the first angel I've met." He turned down a side street and parked at the curb in a parking space with a handicap parking icon painted in it. "Here we are."

I looked around, realizing I had no idea where we were. I hadn't paid attention to his driving, and I didn't recognize the part of the city we were in. Low apartment buildings were crammed together down the road. They weren't falling apart, but they weren't brand new, either, though the trees growing down the street gave the place a pleasant, lived-in air.

We dismounted the van, and Jim led me inside to a first-floor apartment facing the street. "It's not much, but it's home," he said, unlocking the door and gesturing for me to go in first.

The single room was big enough to not feel cramped with Jim's furniture, but with two of us, I could see it becoming so quickly and resolved to try and take up as little of his already meager space as possible.

Other than the size, the first thing I noticed was how clean the space was. Everything seemed to have a place and was in it. The only evidence of any sort of haphazardness were some dishes in the dish drainer. The counters were all lower than the ones I had grown accustomed to in the church's kitchen—likely designed for ease of access. The white, painted walls had pictures strewn across them of people I didn't recognize, but Jim was in several. Some had to have been before his leaving the military because he looked younger and was standing with a group of people, all wearing smiles and holding beer bottles.

I moved out of the way to let Jim in and stepped into what I assumed was his kitchen. The kitchenette had a sink and a small refrigerator along with a two-burner range and meager counter space. His table had three chairs around it with a space for his wheelchair, likely for guests when he had any. A couch acted as a sort of barrier between the living space and Jim's sleeping quarters, and a modest-sized television sat across from it, visible from both the couch and the bed and from an easy chair positioned at an angle to the couch.

Of course, all of this looked like luxury to me since I'd spent a year sleeping on a camping cot in a janitor's closet.

"Make yourself comfortable." Jim gestured toward the furniture. "You can put your things on the table next to the couch if you like."

He smiled at me, and I nodded, feeling an abrupt and terrible sense of awkwardness. While Father John had me visit him at his house on occasion, I hadn't really spent much time there. Unsure of what to do with myself, I shuffled around to sit on the couch, rubbing my hands on my jeans and looking around.

Jim came up next to me and grabbed a remote from the table he'd told me I could put my things on, turning the television on. "You can take a shower if you want. Bathroom's through there." He pointed to a door in the wall off the other end of the couch. "Towels are on the rack. Everything's probably going to be a little low for you, though. Sorry about that." He shrugged.

"Why apologize? This is your home. It should suit you."

Jim shrugged. "You're going to be staying here awhile, and I try to be a good host."

I conjured up something resembling a smile. "You have no need to feel badly about it. I appreciate your help. It is far better than sleeping on the street." I glanced toward the bathroom and decided to take him up on his offer of a shower, if only because I needed a few minutes to myself to sort through everything going on in my head.

Jim settled in to watch the news, occupying the armchair. I set my backpack on the floor beneath the end table and pulled out my body wash and shampoo. He glanced my way for a moment. "You can leave those in the shower if you want. You don't need to carry them around."

"Thank you." I nodded once and passed him, entering the bathroom.

CHAPTER 12

Like the rest of Jim's apartment, the bathroom was exceptionally neat. Jim's toothbrush and razor sat in neat places on the sink alongside a bar of soap in a little dish. He'd been right that everything was low enough that I had to hunch over a bit to reach, but I could tolerate it. At least for a while, anyhow. His shower had a sturdy plastic chair in it that took up most of the space in the tub, and I had to remove it to use the space comfortably.

A small window with frosted glass sat high in the wall, allowing light into the white-tiled room, and I didn't bother flipping on the light switch. It was bright enough to not need it. After a few attempts, I figured out the shower settings and stripped down to get in and started washing down with my body wash.

The hot water felt heavenly, and muscles I hadn't realized were tense began to unwind in the steam. Leaning into the wall, I rested my head on my arm and let the hot water cascade down my back as I tried to sort out my thoughts. It felt as though I were trying to put together a puzzle, but the pieces were from multiple different puzzles, so none of them fit, and I couldn't figure out what the picture was meant to be.

Something in me broke, and a sob I hadn't been prepared for wrenched itself from deep in my chest. Not wanting to disturb Jim, I tried to stay quiet, clamping a hand over my mouth as I wept. I cried for Father John, for my fall, for my confusion, for the loss of my home. Mixed with the grief was fury. That I couldn't save Father John, that Father Demoyne was such an ass, and about a hundred other things.

I didn't know how long I'd been in there, but when I'd finished, I felt lighter somehow. Even if everything ached, and I was exhausted. I turned off the water with trembling fingers and grabbed a towel, wiping my face off and then drying the rest of my body. It felt good to be clean, and I re-dressed in my clothing, unsure what to do with the towel. I thought to ask Jim and spun toward the door and promptly tripped on the shower chair, which sent me crashing into the sink and then onto the floor.

"You okay in there?" Jim's voice came muffled through the door.

"Yes," I said back, picking myself up and glaring at the shower chair before putting it back where it belonged. "I am not harmed."

"All right."

I stepped out of the bathroom, and Jim gave me a once-over. His sharp gaze lingered for a second on my face, but he didn't say anything about whatever it was he saw. "You can put the towel in the hamper over there." He pointed toward the clothes hamper at the foot of his bed. "Feeling any better?"

Whether he meant after my breakdown or after the shower, I didn't know, but I nodded. "Yes." I sunk back down to sit on the couch with a tired sigh.

"Good. Maybe take a nap. I'll call out for dinner in a while. It's kind of been a hell of a day, and I don't feel like cooking."

"All right." I nodded once.

"You like pizza?"

"I will eat almost anything."

"Oh, don't challenge me. I will hold you to that." Jim laughed and gave me a bright grin.

I smiled a little back at him. "I feel like I have made a mistake."

"You have. But me torturing you can wait for a day where we both feel less like hell."

"I appreciate that." I lay out along the couch, resting my head on my arm.

"You can use the blanket on the back if you want. I know I keep it cool in here."

Reaching back, I fumbled for it and dragged a heavy, soft blanket over myself. The weight of it felt reassuring somehow, and I dozed off half-listening to the news. They were talking about the rise of violent crime happening across the city, along with an increase in the presence of a new street drug called "Ripper," but I wasn't paying particular attention and soon drifted off.

Jim woke me by touching my shoulder, and I jumped a little, blinking a few times as I tried to rectify the nightmare I'd been having with the safety and comfort of Jim's apartment. "Pizza's here," he said, patting me and rolling into the kitchen.

I sat up and groaned, stretching and rolling my shoulders. It took me a moment to sort my thoughts as the dregs of the nightmare faded. The details had become hazy the moment I opened my eyes, and all I remembered was a vague sense of helplessness and loss. Nausea and hunger waged a war in my belly, and I got up, resting a hand to my abdomen.

"Try a glass of water to start with," Jim said, gesturing me over to him. He pulled one off a low shelf on the counter. He didn't have much for silverware or plates and such, and what he had seemed to be laid out in easy reach on shelving that ran the length of the back of his rather short counter. It ate into preparatory space, but I guessed that since he lived alone, he didn't need to make the vast quantities I was used to working with in the soup kitchen.

Filling the glass, he passed it over to me, and I downed it in a breath.

"I didn't mean all at once." Jim shook his head and gestured to the table. "If that stays put, pizza's on the table." He rolled over to it and flipped open the box to reveal a pizza covered in hamburger, peppers, mushrooms, and onion. The smell made my stomach growl.

"I cannot tell if it is hunger or nausea." I frowned, sighing.

Jim nodded. "It's a pretty normal thing with everything that's happened the last few days. If you can eat, I suggest it, but I get it if you just can't." He pulled out a piece for himself and picked it up, folding it in half and taking a bite. The look on his face said he regretted it, and he sucked in air, chewing awkwardly.

"Too hot?" I asked, having learned the dangers of too-hot food prior.

"Uh-huh."

"Then perhaps I will wait." I smiled a little and sat down in the chair at the table, staring down at it. "Thank you for the help, Jim. I do not know what I would do without you."

Jim wrestled with his pizza and grabbed a beer out of the fridge, downing part of it before he answered. "Because I warn you when the pizza's hot?"

"That, too." I chuckled and took a piece for myself, finding the nausea had started to subside.

He winked at me. "I've got you, Cass. I keep telling you that. You don't have to face this alone. We'll get through it together."

A sigh left me, but I nodded, taking small bites of the still-too-hot pizza. Jim didn't have much to add while we ate dinner, and when we'd finished, he put the remainder in the fridge, telling me I could get more if I wanted it. By then, the clock on his microwave said it was almost nine. Jim headed into the bathroom to shower before bed, and I wandered the apartment a little, touching nothing. I wasn't even really looking, but the restless energy in me demanded I move, so I paced. I still had no idea how I was going to track this demon down or what my next step was going to be. No matter how many times Jim said we'd figure it out, with no idea what I should be doing, I felt adrift in ways I hadn't since I'd first fallen.

As a warrior by design, not having a battle plan to engage an enemy bothered me. If I were to face a demon in the street, it would be a far easier thing than to deal with an enemy who hid in the shadows and about whom I knew so little. Demons come in many types with powers and knowledge as varied as angels. Some are pathetic, piteous creatures whose existence and focus may be inspiring an excessively specific thing to the detriment of others—say, a demon of smoking a particular brand of cigarettes—just as there are angels whose job it is to watch over the flowers of a designated field in a valley where no human has ever set foot. Others are beings of terrible and awesome power, such as Lucifer himself and those who fell with him.

To my knowledge, few seraphim have fallen from grace since Lucifer's descent from the Heavens. There aren't that many of us to begin with, perhaps a few hundred at the outside. The archangels come from the ranks of the seraphim, each acting as the head of a division, more or less. Michael heads the warriors, Uriel guides the watchers and archivists, and so on. Then there are the cherubim, erelim, ophanim, and on down the line until you reach the malakim, which you'd know as rank and file angels. They mostly serve as messengers between the Heavens and Earth or serve as watchers or chroniclers. Finally, you have the ishim, who are angels in a technical sense but more raw Grace than anything; they serve deeply specific functions, like ensuring gravity does the same thing every time.

Not knowing which choir this demon hailed from meant I couldn't even guess as to its power beyond the chilling knowledge that it was strong enough to walk on sacred ground and enter a church. Which left me to guess it had to be on the higher end of the scales of power. While that wouldn't have given me pause before my fall, now it made me cautious since I had no idea really how much of my power I had retained. And I didn't know how to find out.

As I paced, I gradually became aware of a faint heaviness to the air. I couldn't put my finger on exactly what it was, but something felt off. Wrong. I stopped my restless wandering and looked around the apartment. Nothing struck me as out of place, so I expanded my search to the windows.

Outside, in the center of the street, a figure stood positioned in the patch of shadow between two streetlights. I couldn't see it well in the evening gloom, but I could feel it looking back at me. It was tall, by my perspective, and rather gaunt, though much of anything else was difficult to tell. Whether it was wrapped in the shadows themselves or wearing dark clothing, I didn't know. All I saw was its height and build. That sense of wrongness built in me until I recognized it for what it was: demon.

In a twisted reflection of angelic Grace, demons have something we refer to as "Blight." It's not the same word in Enochian, but that's the closest translation. Where Grace is the building block of creation, Blight is the power demons possess to match it. It fuels their power, and just as they can feel the presence of Grace, so too can angels feel Blight. The more powerful a source of it, the harder it is to hide, and the feel of the demon's Blight from this distance told me this was at least enough of a threat to warrant notice.

We stood in silence, sizing one another up for an eternity before a car passed down the street, shining its headlights into the space where the figure had been. Nothing. The heaviness vanished as light filled the street, and the car passed. Was it the demon that had killed Father John? Or was it another? Perhaps a minion. Revealing itself to me had been a ploy of some kind, of that I was certain. But what kind, I didn't know.

Just then, the bathroom door opened, and Jim came into the living area, rubbing a towel over his head. He wore nothing but a pair of loose sweatpants that had been cut off at about the length of his legs. His chest and shoulders remained broad and muscular despite having been out of the military for years, but I didn't really study him, expecting he'd find it rude. It would also likely have been awkward for both of us. I suspected he spent a fair amount of time and energy on keeping his strength. Soldiers—myself included—seemed to be of that mindset.

He paused in the middle of drying his hair and lowered the towel. "What?"

In that moment I decided not to tell him what I'd seen since I didn't have any idea what it could mean. I shook my head. "Thought I saw something outside." While not exactly a lie, the untruth tasted bitter on my tongue.

Jim watched me for a second before nodding and going back to his drying. He then headed over to the bed and pulled himself up onto it, flopping across the mattress with a weary sigh. "I'm gonna crash. You can watch TV if you want. It won't keep me up."

"Thank you, Jim." I nodded to him and sunk back down to sit on the couch.

CHAPTER 13

The next morning, Jim woke me up early by closing the bathroom door. He did so quietly, but any noise was enough to stir the restless slumber I'd fallen into sometime after dawn had broken. I'd lain awake staring at the ceiling most of the night.

I sat up, rubbing my tired, dry eyes and swung my legs off the couch, resting my elbows on my knees for a moment before I ambled into the kitchen and took the glass I'd used the night before out of the drainer. I filled it with water from the tap, downing it before I rinsed it and set the glass where it had been and leaned on the counter for a minute.

Jim came out of the bathroom and rolled into the kitchen. "Got cold pizza, eggs, and cereal if you want 'em."

"Thank you." I rubbed my hands over my face again. "Did you sleep well?"

"Slept fine. We've got some stuff at the church tonight, I know, but I was thinking we could do something this afternoon. Get you out of your head a little. You game?" Jim pulled a jug of milk out of his refrigerator and collected cereal, a bowl, and a spoon from the counter and one of the cupboards.

I took him up on his offer of cold pizza, and we sat down at his table for breakfast. "I guess? I do not know what there is to do. Father John did not take me out much. He was very busy."

Jim waved at me with his spoon. "I know. Figure it's time you actually got to see some of the city you live in rather than just the church. If you're going to live down here, you should learn the place."

It made sense to the tactical side of me. Knowing the lay of the land meant I could plan more effectively. "All right."

The two of us ate, and when we'd finished, Jim and I took turns getting changed in the bathroom before he took us outside where he headed down the block, passing his van. Instead, we made our way to the T station nearby.

"Why do you not wish to drive?" I asked, tilting my head a little.

"There's a station right near where we're going. I drive to the church because I'm usually hauling coffee, donuts, paperwork, and all that fun stuff. Carrying that on the T as a guy in a wheelchair? No thanks. Today, it's just us. Besides, there's construction on Storrow. Again. So the surface streets are going to be a catastrophe between here and where we're going."

He said the words like I had any idea what he was talking about. I didn't know what Storrow was, but I nodded anyway, guessing it was a road based on context. "Where are we going?"

"Somewhere." He led me into the Copley T station, about a mile away from the apartment, and paid for my fare. The T was, to me, remarkable. While it was loud and smelled like diesel fumes, the fact that they could move so many people so quickly through the city had never ceased to amaze me.

On the crowded platform, a tired-looking tusked man sat on one of the benches. His clothes suggested blue-collar work, maybe day labor of some kind. I didn't know. He had a large coffee clutched in one, broad hand, and his eyes were half-closed. He took up most of the bench based on the sheer size of him. Maybe a troll? I didn't know the tusked races well enough to be sure. Dust had explained that they were all closely related, but of the three tusked races—orcs, ogres, and trolls—trolls were the biggest. And this man fit the bill.

An elf—or maybe a fae, I couldn't tell—woman wearing a tailor-made suit walked up and stood in front of him with an annoyed expression. I couldn't hear their exchange, but her gestures told me she was probably demanding he get up and give her his seat. He refused, as might be expected, and the two started an argument in earnest.

I went to head over toward them to try and stop the fight, but Jim grabbed my wrist. "Nope. Best you let them sort that out themselves. He doesn't look like he needs help."

"Why are they fighting?"

"It's complicated. Probably racism, if I'm honest. Lots of folks think less of the tusked races. They've been treated badly for a long time, and there's a lot of bad blood between the tusked and the elves. You could ask Eirlas—he knows more than I do. But the tusked are treated like crap a lot of the time. It's not all of 'em, and not all the time. Dust and Eirlas, for example, get along just fine, but it's just a thing you'll see. It's not something that's ever sat well with me."

"I do not understand."

"I wouldn't think you would. Racism probably doesn't make much sense to you."

"No. You are all children of God and beloved to Him. It is like siblings fighting over who their father likes better when their father loves them both the same."

"It's more complex than that, but... this isn't the time or the place for me to explain it. But you are correct that the Father loves us all the same."

I would have asked more, but the subway train arrived, and we all filed forward. I stood near Jim, putting my hands in my pockets. Something stabbed my right thumb, and I jumped, pulling my hand out again and staring at the little spot of blood on my finger. The bleeding stopped almost immediately, and I carefully reached back in to discover the little cocktail umbrella I'd taken from the table at the bar.

"What good are angels?"

My throat tightened a little, and I swallowed against the sensation, curling my fingers around the umbrella and letting out a slow, deep breath. The umbrella was a little ratty from having been in the pocket of these pants for almost a week, but I didn't know what else to do with it, so I returned it there.

Jim was watching the other people in the train car with us, his eyes never really settling on anyone for long, and if he'd noticed my moment with the umbrella, he didn't say anything about it. I took it as a mercy, since I didn't want to try and explain to him what had happened.

The rest of the ride was uneventful. When our stop came, Jim led me out the doors and toward the elevator, where we rode it up and disembarked out onto State Street. The air smelled different there. Sort of salty in a way I couldn't identify, and I sniffed at it, though I struggled to pick it apart from the scents of the T station. As we walked through yet another part of the city I had not been to, it struck me then just how large the world had to be.

I hadn't spent much time beyond the walls of the church, so the sheer scope of it hadn't entirely sunk in yet. My pace slowed a little as I looked upward at the tall buildings above us when we emerged from the underground. "How big is the city?"

"That's a question for Google," Jim said, pausing and pulling out his phone. "According to this, eighty-nine point six three miles squared."

"I have no idea how big that is," I said with a frown.

"You know the park outside the church?"

I nodded.

"That's about a quarter a mile from end to end."

My brows rose, and that sense of smallness deepened. "Oh."

"I didn't bring you here to stare at the buildings. C'mon." Jim led me down the sidewalk until the buildings parted. From there, I could see more sky than I had yet seen. The building we were approaching was quite large, but to the left and right of it was a vastness of nothing. Not entirely understanding what I was looking at, I stopped. That strange, salty smell filled my nose, and I tried to figure out what in the world I was looking at.

"That's the ocean, Cass. The Atlantic, to be specific. And this," he pointed to the large structure, "is the New England Aquarium."

I tilted my head. "What is an ah-kwer-ee-um?" I sounded out the word awkwardly as we made our way to the front doors.

"You'll see. I think you'll enjoy it." He gave me a grin.

As we approached, to the left, I paused at an enclosure with several, large, brown animals in it who made odd, barking noises at me when I approached. Jim chuckled and identified them as harbor seals. We stood there for a few moments, watching them, before he guided me inside. He paid for admission, and we then entered the aquarium proper.

If you have never been to the New England Aquarium, it is a beautiful place filled with fascinating exhibits, the highlights of which are the penguin exhibit (which I spent a very long time admiring) and the massive multi-story coral reef tank. A long ramp wrapped around the tank, and the outer walls lined with tanks contained many beautiful and interesting fish, but the main tank drew my attention in ways the side ones couldn't hold.

Jim and I made our way around the length of the place with me stopping every few moments to point out a fish of some kind to him, and the first time I saw a shark glide by the glass, I could hardly believe the size of it. Living in the city as I did, I had not seen much for wildlife beyond the usual city birds—seagulls, pigeons, crows, sparrows, and the like—and squirrels in the park. I'd been around dogs on occasion, but this was an entirely different scale.

We explored the aquarium for several hours before Jim brought me out to the cafeteria and purchased a meal for us, and we sat together at a small table with hot dogs, chips, and soda. While we ate, I babbled to him about the fish we had seen, and Jim listened with infinite patience. Looking back on it, he probably enjoyed my enthusiasm and joy much the same as others enjoy the chatter of an excited child.

When we'd finished eating, he let me wander with him through the place a second time before we left. I didn't really want to go, but we had to go to the church to do our jobs and tend to the needs of others.

"I'm glad you had such a good time, Cass. I wanted to show you that not everything is awful. Even if we are dealing with some difficult things, there is still beauty in the world. And there's a lot more than just that. I'll take you to the zoo sometime and let you see the animals there. And then there's the Museum of Fine Arts. And the Museum of Science. And plenty of other places." He took my hand in his and squeezed firmly. "Things might seem bleak sometimes, but there's a lot of good out there. You just have to know to look for it."

He released my fingers, and we took the T back to the stop near Jim's apartment where we mounted up in his van and headed toward the church. For the first time since Father John had died, I felt almost normal. And for a little while, I was able to let go of the worries about demons lurking in the darkness, my friend's death, and the looming question of what I was going to do about it.

CHAPTER 14

Jim parked in the parking lot near the church, and we both got out. "You going to help me get set up for my group before you head down to the kitchen to help Dust?" Jim asked as I walked alongside him toward the door.

"Of course."

"You could stay for the group if you wanted to, you know."

"I am not a soldier in any war the people you work with would understand." I frowned.

Jim looked up at me. "Not the same way I was, but... you were. You had orders and were expected to maintain them. You saw combat. You've got more in common with them, and me, than you might think."

I considered his words. They made some sense to me, but I still questioned how much I could have in common with mortal creatures. What would I say, anyway? *Hi, I am Cassiel, an angel of the Lord. I was foolish and disobeyed and was cast down.* I shook my head, dispelling the thought. "Maybe sometime, Jim. But not tonight. I need to help Dust cook. He is expecting me."

"All right. Well... Tuesdays and Thursdays every week are when we meet. Make some time."

We reached the church, and I followed him upstairs and set up the six or so chairs and got coffee brewing. While his group consisted of himself and four others regularly, Jim always insisted on having extra chairs out in case someone else joined them. Likewise, he provided extra coffee, creamer, and sugar.

When I'd finished helping him prepare, we parted ways with the understanding that we'd meet in the soup kitchen when I'd finished serving. I left the main building and walked across the small courtyard to the soup kitchen, entering in through the kitchen door.

Dust noticed me first and nodded sharply in my direction. He didn't smile much, but I'd grown to understand his ways. I waved a little to him. When the other volunteers turned to acknowledge me, they stood silent for a minute until Dust barked at them to get back to what they were doing. I paused, lingering near the door as an overwhelming desire to leave stripped away the joy I had experienced with Jim earlier.

Stomping over to me, Dust pointed to one of the sinks. "Well? Get to it, Cass. We've got a lot to do." He leaned a little closer then, speaking quietly. "Don't let 'em get to you." He then patted my shoulder with a heavy thump and got back to his duties.

I took a slow breath and tried to steel myself before heading to the sink and washing up before I approached Dust. He set me to peeling potatoes, something I had done many times for him. The repetition of it soothed me somehow, and by the time I had finished peeling the veritable mountain of them, I was no longer worried about the eyes on me. With the potatoes all peeled, Dust started me on dicing them for mashed potatoes, slicing up one and showing me the size he wanted.

Of all the things cooking requires, using a knife is the most comfortable for me. While I lack the practiced precision Dust has, holding a knife feels as natural to me as breathing. It may not be being used as a weapon, but it still is one, and I can use them to produce the desired effect with more ease than I wield other kitchen implements.

When I'd finished my task, Dust set me to making salad. Then I helped load things into the steam table trays and brought them out front to where the servers were giving out plates to anyone who approached them. I loaded and unloaded the trays as they finished serving portions of them out for the better part of half an hour until Dust shooed me out front to go eat.

I joined the people in the main room of the soup kitchen and plucked a tray from the end of the line. The kitchen was laid out more or less like a buffet, but instead of serving yourself, someone else served your portions to you to ensure everyone got a fair serving.

The room itself seats maybe a hundred patrons at large, round tables. Most of the furnishings have seen better days, but they still do their jobs, and the volunteers keep the place immaculately clean. The cracked, weathered floor tiles look like they'd come out of the 1970s when the place had been built, and the ceiling is missing a tile or two in a few places.

I sat down at a table near Mary Beth, offering her a smile. My heart sunk to see her still frequenting this place after well over a week, but it wasn't an unusual pattern for her from what I'd learned over the last year. "Good evening, Mary Beth."

Mary Beth had frizzy brown hair, too-large glasses, freckles across her nose, and a mousy sort of way about her. Her ears came to rounded points, suggesting some kind of elven heritage, but she had the wrong facial features for it to be more than half. She glanced up at me over the top of the book she was reading. I didn't recognize the title, but the cover had a dragon and a scantily clad woman on it. The woman wielded a sword, but her armor looked, frankly, useless.

"Hello, Cass." Mary Beth spoke with a slight lisp, something I had been told she was very shy about. Typically, she dressed in clothing several sizes too big for her—something I suspected was an attempt to hide the bruises I'd seen on her arms. She never talked about where they came from, but everyone at the shelter suspected they were from her father.

I tilted my head. "That outfit is not very protective. She should find something better to wear into battle."

Mary Beth chuckled. "I guess, yeah. I didn't really think about it." She stuck a finger in between the pages to keep her place and looked at the cover. "She ends up romancing the dragon, so it's not really about combat."

"Then why is she holding a sword?"

"Because she's supposed the slay the dragon and—"

"So she should be wearing more clothes!" I shook my head. "It is poor tactics to go into battle wearing such a garment. I do not understand it."

Shaking her head, Mary Beth laughed. "It's just a costume. It's not supposed to really be armor or anything."

"If one is representing combat, they should be properly armed." I grunted and stabbed a fork into my chicken and rice. "It is a bad choice."

She continued laughing. "You're so weird. It's just a novel, not like… a tactical manual or anything." Mary Beth dogeared the page and put her book down on the table, paying some attention to her dinner. "I'm sorry about Father John. He was really nice. I'm gonna miss him."

"He is with the Father in Heaven now. I will miss him as well, but he is at peace." I took a couple bites of my food, but the subject had done irreparable harm to my appetite. "But I appreciate your con… consoles?"

"Condolences," Mary Beth corrected, having some of her water. "I think that's the word you're looking for."

I nodded in response since my mouth was full. Even after a year in the world, I still possessed an extremely limited vocabulary and often struggled. "How long are you staying with us this time, Mary Beth? Not that I mind you being here, or have any say in it, but you have been here over a week now." I kept my tone as casual as I could and focused my attention on my food, watching her out of the corner of my eye.

Mary Beth's face fell, and her shoulders hunched a little. "I dunno. Dad just said he was leaving on business for a while. I don't even know where he went. If I have to leave to make room for someone else, I can."

"That was not what I meant. I just wished to know what was going on in your life. You are here often, and I dislike seeing you treated the way you are. I want to help."

Her mouth pulled to the side a bit. "I like you, Cass. You say what you think. You don't really beat around the bush or anything."

"Why would I strike a bush?"

Mary Beth chuckled. "It's just a saying. I dunno. It means to kind of not say what you mean directly."

"I do not see how those things are related, but I will take you at your word." Understanding turns of phrase had been a sore spot of mine, something Father John had been working on with me before he died. Until I understood the origins of the saying, I struggled to make sense of them, and even if I did understand the origins, I still, at times, couldn't put the pieces together.

Mary Beth nudged peas around her plate. "I'm not sure there's anything you can really do to help, though. Just… gotta live my life, yanno? Sometimes you don't always get a say in everything that happens to you." She sighed. "Ever since Mom died, my dad's been weird. All these trips'n stuff. He never used to go away so much."

I reached over to her and put my hand on her wrist. "You do not always get a say in what has happened, but you get to decide what you do with it. That is one of the things Father John taught me." I smiled a little and squeezed her wrist before releasing it.

A look I couldn't quite understand crossed her face, and Mary Beth nodded with a sigh. "Yeah." She seemed to me like she wanted to say something else, but before she could, a shout near the front door drew my attention.

I was halfway to my feet before I'd processed what was happening. A gaunt-looking elven man with wide, bloodshot eyes stood in the doorway, holding something I identified as a large firearm of some kind. A rifle, perhaps? I didn't know all the names for them yet, despite Father John having talked to me a bit about them when we watched the news and saw clips of wars in far-off countries. His clothes looked rumpled and unwashed, and his hair hung in greasy strands around his still-handsome face.

The world faded into what felt like slow motion as I grabbed Mary Beth and lifted the table, flipping it upright with a crash of cutlery as chaos erupted around us. I shoved her down behind the table and put my hand on her head, trying to get her as low to the ground as possible. "Stay here," I hissed, manifesting my two primary wings.

She stared at me with eyes wide and afraid but nodded. Her lips were pale, and the pupils tiny pinpricks against the brown of her irises. I squeezed her shoulder to try and reassure her, though I didn't say anything.

I took a couple breaths before I got up and walked around the edge of the table, straight into the man's line of fire.

CHAPTER 15

ey! That is enough!" I yelled, opening my wings as wide as I could. I don't remember where, but at some point, I had learned that some animals, when threatened, tried to make themselves look bigger so a potential enemy would back down. If nothing else, I thought it might draw his attention and make me a target rather than those less prepared.

His watering, bloodshot gray eyes swung toward me, and he lifted the gun in my direction. The veins on his neck stood out, and sweat poured down his pale face, making him look somewhere between sick and crazed. His finger tightened on the trigger, and the firearm roared.

I'd never heard a sound that loud in my life, and I reeled a little in instinctive response before charging him. I didn't think the shot had hit me, but I didn't wait to find out. Whatever happened to me didn't matter; I couldn't let him harm the people who were screaming and ducking for cover wherever they could behind me. "Stop this. What is the point of such an act?"

I was almost in arm's reach when I saw his hand tense again, finger tightening to pull the trigger. The shot never came.

Jim came barreling down the side hallway that led from the soup kitchen into the rest of the building. "What in the name of God's glorious green creation do you think you are *doing*, boy?" he barked, his tone all at once authoritative and demanding. "Did I give you the authorization to pull that trigger? You will stand down and follow orders when you are facing a superior officer. Do I make myself clear?" He drew himself up so tall and straight in his chair, pointing at the elf in a manner that, frankly, intimidated *me*, and I wasn't on the receiving end of it. "Now, you *will* stop with the games, safe that weapon, and sit your ass on that floor until told otherwise!"

The elf turned toward him, the hand with the firearm swinging in his direction just as my momentum carried me into him and slammed him into the door. I grabbed the firearm and yanked it away from him with very little effort, ejecting the magazine and chambered round without really thinking about it. The weapon was part of me for that moment, and I knew everything I needed to know about it. Weapons were one of the few things that made perfect, clear sense to me, and I didn't need to think to comprehend them. I could let my hands do their work and keep my attention on other things.

In that moment where I was removing the firearm as a threat, the elf squirmed away from me, rushing toward Jim. I dropped the gun to go help him, but in that space of time, Jim had pulled a handheld black box from somewhere I hadn't noticed, and as soon as his assailant closed on him, he rammed it into the other man's ribs.

There was a buzzing, cracking sound, and the elf started making noises I couldn't quite quantify for a few seconds before collapsing to the ground. I didn't have much time to register what had happened before the door beside me opened to admit a second person, also with the same wild look in their eyes. This time it was a woman, and she, too, had a gun. Albeit a much smaller one. She stood just outside my reach, the weapon trained on me as she looked around the place. "Connor!" she yelled, her voice high and tight.

I shook my head, crowding her space a little while keeping my wings splayed to block her view of everyone else in the space. "Put down the gun," I said, keeping my voice as calm as I could. I still couldn't reach the firearm, and if she chose to pull that trigger, I doubted she'd miss. "There is no need for that here. Nobody is going to hurt you."

"Where's Connor?" she demanded, punctuating the statement by thrusting the gun at me as though it would make it more dangerous.

"I do not know who Connor is, so I do not know where he is."

"He's my… He's all that matters!"

I moved toward her slowly, trying to get in range to take the weapon from her, but I kept my hands forward and up. While I'm not a good liar, and have never been, the feint was well within my power. "I see. Perhaps if you put down the gun, we can find him together?"

She yelled something incoherent and stepped forward. Her body language warned me she was about to fire, so I closed on her, grabbing the firearm and pushing it upward to point at the ceiling. In the same moment, a line of fiery pain erupted along the side of my head that almost made me let go, but I managed to fight through it and held her arms up as she emptied the magazine into the ceiling.

When she'd unloaded the gun, I used the full force of my strength to crush it in my hand. While it didn't fall apart or any such thing, it was definitely no longer usable. I had damaged the barrel and slide enough that they would no longer move over one another and allow the weapon to fire. Not without exploding.

The woman continued to scream, releasing the gun and launching herself at me to try and claw at me. While I caught one hand, she got me across the face with the other before I could control her flailing limbs. The scratches hurt, but they had done no real damage. However, the wound along the side of my scalp bled heavily. Wet heat poured down my face and neck into my shirt collar and dripped off my chin to the floor, making the tired old yellow tile slick.

Even with her arms held, she tried to bite at me like a feral beast, and somewhere in her frantic, crazed eyes, I caught a glimpse of something. I couldn't quite place it, but some part of me recognized the expression on instinct. I didn't linger on the thought, continuing to try and fend her off until Jim rolled over and used his black box on her. When he did, I yelped and let go almost instantly as the force of a great deal of electricity slammed through where I held her into my hands. The moment I released her, the sensation lessened.

She collapsed to the floor unmoving, and I sagged a little, the adrenaline starting to give way to pain as blood poured over my skin. I put a hand out and leaned on the wall to steady myself as dizziness filled me.

Jim touched my elbow. "Let me see." He then turned his head, bellowing into the room. "Somebody get me a towel. Now!" His tone returned to that harsh, sharp one he'd used on the first attacker, though it softened when he addressed me again. "Sit down, Cass. Sit down before you fall."

I obeyed, sinking to the floor and closing my eyes. "Room's spinning," I said, my voice coming out as a slur. That, and I felt a bone-deep cold swallow me. My muscles tensed and shivered. Something touched my head, and I jumped, grabbing for the thing with abrupt force. My hand found a forearm, and I gripped into it with the points of my fingers, seeking for control.

Despite it having to hurt, Jim didn't pull the towel away from my head. "You're okay, soldier. I've got you. Help's coming. Just breathe, Cassiel. Breathe."

When I realized who and what it was, I let go and tried to follow Jim's advice, but despite the slow, deep breaths, my heart felt like it was going to pound out of my chest. My head hurt so much I worried I'd vomit. I had only done that a couple times and didn't relish the idea of doing so again.

The piercing wail of a siren outside made me grimace, and I became dimly aware of people descending on us, but the commotion washed over me in a tremendous blend of roaring sound. I have vague memories of Jim telling me he'd follow me soon—whatever that meant—and then nothing.

The next thing I remember was waking in a hospital again and aching more or less everywhere. My head felt like it had been split open with an axe. On instinct, I lifted a hand to touch it, perhaps to confirm it was still all there. My fingers found gauze and medical tape, and apparently, they had shaved a good part of my hair, which annoyed me. I'd needed a haircut, but not like that.

I didn't have long to try and put things together before Jim entered, escorted by a nurse. I tried to sit up but regretted the motion immediately and went still until the room stopped spinning again. "Jim?"

"I'm here. You got a bunch of staples and a nasty concussion, but you're going to heal just fine. They tell me you're going to be clear to leave as soon as you get your head together." Jim moved over to the left side of my bed and took my hand into his. "How're you feeling?"

"I hurt." An understatement. "What happened to them?"

"The people who attacked us?"

"Yes."

Jim nodded slowly. "They're in the hospital here and will be going into police custody soon. Sounds like they both were overdosing on Ripper." He squeezed my hand. "You saved a lot of people yesterday."

"Good. Was anyone hurt?"

"Only you. Listen, now that you're awake, the police are going to want to talk to you. They know you didn't do anything wrong, so you're not in trouble for this. They're just going to try and understand from you what happened, okay?"

I nodded a little, the motion making the room swim some, but the longer I was awake, the more clearheaded I felt. "All right. Will you stay?"

"I don't think they'll let me be in here when they question you, Cass. But I'll be right outside." His thumb grazed my knuckles with firm pressure. It reassured me somehow.

Which brought me to another thought, and I sat up a little on my elbows, trying to ignore the swirling sensation in my gut. "Your arm. Did I hurt you?"

"I've got some interesting bruises, but you didn't do any real damage. It's okay. I knew something like that might happen. Don't worry about it right now." Jim put a hand to the center of my chest and pushed, encouraging me to lie back. "We'll get you home soon."

CHAPTER 16

I left the hospital a few hours later after answering a hundred questions from uniformed officers about the shooting. While they weren't particularly unkind to me, they didn't seem to really want to be there. And given my status as a potential murder suspect, I doubted they trusted much of what I had to say. Apparently, though, what I told them matched with what everyone else who had been there said enough that they were satisfied with my account of events.

Retelling the story made me remember that look in the woman's eyes when I'd been wrestling with her, and something down in me resonated with it, but my head hurt too much for me to put all the pieces together. All I knew was something in there struck me as familiar somehow. It had stuck with me despite how much of what happened felt more like a blur than actual events. They told me that was common for traumatic events and I might remember more later. If I did, I was to tell them.

When the police had finished with me, Jim returned, and a doctor joined him. The doctor told me I had been "grazed" by the bullet and had twelve staples down the side of my head. He then explained how to care for them and pressed a bag of gauze, medical tape, and some kind of ointment into my hands. I was released a short time later into Jim's care.

By then, I could walk on my own and had answered enough questions about what day it was and so on that they were satisfied that my mind was functional. Honestly, I was grateful to leave that place. It brought back far too many memories of Father John, and the sensation of lying helpless in a hospital bed while a demon terrorized the city didn't sit well with me.

Jim drove me back to his apartment and sat me on the couch. "All right, let's get you settled in. Dust wants to come by and check on you when he gets out of work. He's fretting like a mother hen and has been since you went in."

It struck me as odd that Dust would worry so much about anything, but I didn't argue. My head hurt like someone had… well… shot me. After two times in the hospital now, I had discovered that my inability to be affected by alcohol extended to drugs—including painkillers. Which meant they'd had to knock me unconscious with magic, or so I'd been told. While magic works in place of anesthesia in cases like mine, it requires a practitioner to be present and casting during the entire procedure, which is exhausting, and for long operations, switching out practitioners is an extremely delicate thing to ensure both the patient doesn't wake up or, of course, die.

However, the inability to use painkillers meant that, at the moment, I felt horrible. Every inch of the bullet wound to the side of my head throbbed with pain, and my whole head ached. Jim rolled over and pulled the blanket off the back of the couch, putting it across my lap. "You want to watch TV or just sit quietly?" he asked, keeping his voice low.

"I want answers," I said with a deep sigh. "Who were those two people? What did they want? Why were they acting like that?"

"I can't answer all those questions, but I can tell you they were high. The police said it was ripper. So, if I had to guess, I'd probably say they didn't even know what they wanted."

"I have heard that word several times. What is 'Ripper?'"

"It's a drug. Like cocaine or methamphetamine."

I frowned. Father John had explained drugs to me, but I couldn't grasp their appeal. All I knew was some people used them to alter their minds. Some I understood, like morphine or marijuana. They helped with pain or assisted people to function. But the ones he called "recreational" were what I couldn't grasp. Part of it was likely because I couldn't experience the sensations, and the concept of escape hadn't been something I understood at the time. "I heard about cocaine, heroin, methamphetamine, and others, but I do not remember Father John telling me about ripper."

Jim shook his head. "It's pretty new. It's only been on the street a couple months. From what I understand, it does something to remove inhibitions. You ever hear of berserkers?"

I shook my head.

"Berserkers were these ancient warriors who went into frenzy in battle. Things that would've stopped most people didn't even slow 'em down. They're like weres in that way except they don't change forms or anything. They're just people."

"Yes." That, I understood. Therianthropes—commonly referred to as "weres" by slang—have the capacity to frenzy if pushed far enough. Those frenzies are devastating things given the propensity of weres to lose themselves in feral fury and being possessed of the ability to heal themselves rapidly and be far stronger than most races on average. An ogre or troll could probably go toe-to-toe with one and make it out the other side with the right kind of training, but anything weaker than that would likely be torn to shreds without specialized training, weaponry, and luck.

"That's what ripper does, so far as I know. Eirlas might know more about the specifics since he's really… well versed in that kind of thing." Jim hedged a little on talking about Eirlas' relationship with drugs, and after the eulogy he'd given, I understood some of why. Still, I intended to ask Eirlas about what had happened the next time I saw him.

I closed my eyes with a sigh. "I am just glad I was there, and no one was seriously hurt."

"Says the woman with a dozen staples in her head." Jim's voice sounded somewhere between amused and annoyed.

"I will heal. I heal faster than most of you down here." I waved a hand in response. "And I can likely take more damage before I am felled."

Jim grunted. "Well, having seen you in action, I more or less believe it. But that doesn't mean I'm not going to take that head wound seriously. You should, too. It's nothing to laugh at. You're compromised, Cass. It's a tactical disadvantage."

Despite my reticence to admit it, Jim was right. That didn't make me any happier about it, and I frowned a little. "I suppose. Do you think that attack on the church was related to Father John's death?"

"Maybe. I don't know. I need to call Dust—we'll finish this in a few minutes, all right?" He patted my shoulder and rolled off into the kitchen to give me, and him, the illusion of privacy while he made the call.

I sat in silence while he spoke with Dust, plucking at the blanket he'd put across me. At least no one else had been hurt in that whole catastrophe. Whether it had anything to do with the demon's attack on the church bothered me. Overall, demons tend to be extremely calculating creatures. They plan, plot, design, and work from the shadows, pulling strings. They aren't typically out in the open because it exposes them in ways many of them prefer to not be seen and can also alert those who are able to fight them.

Angels are not the only creatures capable of facing off against demons. The faithful and trained can condemn, expel, and drive off demons. While faith acts as a shield against them—true faith, not just casual attendance—it will only go so far when something is bringing down claws on your face. That said, the church, over the millennia since the Son's presence on Earth, has collected those capable of such feats. Heaven has tapped others beyond the church's influence, of course, but I knew I wasn't the only creature in the world capable of handling this problem.

Of course, none of this knowledge did me any good since I didn't know how to find any of those people.

I went to run my fingers through my hair as it had become a nervous habit and bashed my stapled scalp, which drew a hiss of pain. Jim paused his conversation to speak up in my direction. "You okay over there?"

"Yes." I nodded. "Just touched a place that hurts."

Jim nodded once and went back to talking with Dust, leaving me to my thoughts.

Assuming this was an archdemon, and assuming it had been the same one I'd seen outside the apartment here the other night, it wouldn't be working alone. For all there is a fair amount of infighting in the demonic ranks, they have a rigid hierarchy, and I knew an archdemon working in the city would have underlings—and some of those underlings might even be human. That is one of their favorite tactics: making non-celestial creatures act for them. It means they can stand back in the shadows and watch without risking themselves directly to the aforementioned forces of Heaven.

Of course, were we really much different? Heaven had been calling to mortal beings down below to do its bidding just the same as demons had. Maybe it was my perspective as a fallen, but it felt a little like being a piece in the world's largest strategy game. And I wasn't an extremely important piece, either, so at any moment, I could be moved into a position to be sacrificed for the greater strategy. The idea rested heavily on me, and I looked over at Jim, realizing that he faced the same fate with even less understanding than I did.

I didn't resent the Father for this. I couldn't. His plan and will were absolute, and I knew I had to trust in them, but that didn't make being a proverbial pawn any more comfortable.

CHAPTER 17

Jim and I rested that evening, and we didn't do much talking. I could see wheels turning in his head, just as he must have seen them in mine, but neither of us shared those thoughts with the other, instead favoring silence. It wasn't an uneasy quiet, but with us both too wrapped up in our own worries, there wasn't enough air in the room for conversation.

At some point during the evening, Jim turned on the television, and we watched the news. It seemed to be his go-to. He eventually dozed off in his recliner, and I lay staring at the ceiling until fatigue overwhelmed me.

The next morning, I woke with a gasp from nightmares I couldn't quite recall when I opened my eyes. The sound must have stirred Jim because all at once, he was bolt upright and reaching for something, but his hands only found the arms of the recliner he'd fallen asleep in. We stared at each other for a moment as our minds worked to collect themselves, and then we relaxed.

"Hey, uh… This might be kind of awkward, but you need help getting cleaned up? I can wash your hair for you if you want. You can do the rest, but I know with a head wound like that, getting your hair clean is going to be impossible on your own."

I considered the offer but nodded eventually. "Yes. I think that would be helpful. I am not supposed to get it wet."

"Yeah, I know a bit about that." He gestured to his legs. "S'why I offered. Also, I know being clean after all that will be probably the best thing you've ever experienced. We can put the shower chair outside the tub, and I can sit on that while I do your hair for you. Once I'm done with your hair, I'll leave you to do the rest on your own. Though… if it's just the same, I'm going to sit in there with you. With a concussion like yours, I want to make sure you don't pass out or anything."

"Thank you." I nodded and got up, finding the worst of the dizziness from the day before had faded. While my head still felt foggy and my eyes didn't want to focus well, I felt better than I had. Fortunately, I healed quickly. While for a human, the head wound would take six to eight weeks to heal—or so they'd said at the hospital—I had recovered from the damage to my neck and chest in a matter of days. This led the people at the hospital to label me as "meta–unknown species" in my discharge paperwork, or so Father John had told me.

Meta is the catch-all term referring to anything with latent magical abilities due to their race. The tusked races, elves, humans, centaurs, satyrs, and other such races without innate magical abilities aren't considered meta, while races such as vampires, therianthropes, fae, and so on have latent magical abilities that give them their power.

I walked into the bathroom and moved the shower chair out beside the tub before stripping off my clothes and turning on the hot water. Once it was the right temperature, I climbed into the tub and moved the spray so it wasn't directly on me.

"You ready?" Jim asked from the doorway. I could tell he was trying to give me as much privacy as possible, but nudity didn't much bother me. What need had I to be ashamed?

"Yes."

He came into the room and maneuvered himself onto the shower chair before taking the detachable head of the shower and carefully and gently wetting my hair down, avoiding the wound. He then set to washing my hair for me while I sat with my head bowed and let him work. When Jim finished, he patted my shoulder. "All good. I'll leave you to the rest." He closed the shower curtain to afford me privacy, and I stood, leaning against the wall for a moment. The heat made my head hurt worse, but my muscles enjoyed the steamy water.

I cleaned myself and stood for as long as I thought I could tolerate under the spray. Through the shower curtain, I could see Jim's shadow transfer back to his wheelchair and, as he'd promised, he sat quietly while I finished cleaning up. When I turned the water off, he pulled the shower curtain aside a little to hand me a towel.

"Thank you."

"You're welcome. If you need help, let me know, but your head's hurt, not your hands, so I didn't figure you'd need it."

"You are right." I dried off, very carefully blotting the area around my wound. Being clean felt rejuvenating in ways I didn't have words for at that moment, and I resolved to thank him after I'd dressed.

He left the room and returned with my backpack. "You've got clean clothes here. I'm going to step out and let you dress. Seems like you've got everything okay."

"I do. Thank you again." I finished drying off and waited for him to leave before I dressed in a pair of worn jeans and a black t-shirt. When I was done, I glanced in the mirror, looking at the long, puckered wound down the length of my scalp. At least it wasn't bleeding, but I was curious to know if it would scar like the wounds from the demon had. I looked at the claw marks down my neck and chest and traced them with my fingers. They stood as permanent reminders of what had happened. Of my mistake.

Like I could forget it.

At least they no longer ached. And, for the most part, my clothes hid them, so people didn't tend to ask questions or even really notice them. It was just as well since I'd seen how they looked at others with such marks.

I turned away from my reflection and opened the bathroom door. Jim had changed while I did, wearing similar clothing. Though his shirt was gray and had the word "Marines" across the front of it. He gave me a smile. "You feeling better?"

I nodded, smiling a little in return. "Yes. Thank you. You were right about the shower. I feel much better."

"Good. Look, I've got to head in to the church for a while and do some paperwork. You can stay here if you want, but I'd kind of rather have you where I can keep an eye on you. Are you comfortable coming in with me?"

"I should be all right. My head hurts if I move too much, but if I sit in the common space, it should be all right."

"Good. I'll get us breakfast on the way. You ready to go?"

I nodded, and Jim and I left. On the way to the church, good on his word, he drove through a Dunkin's and got us breakfast sandwiches and coffee. I had learned to appreciate coffee with Father John. While I didn't feel any such rush of energy or alertness as he described after drinking it, I enjoyed the taste and found the warmth comforting. Jim also picked up donuts and hot coffee for the church on his way through.

We ate on the road, and Jim pulled us up to the church. The drive had taken us a little over half an hour, and by then, I had shaken off the dregs of the dream while listening to Jim growl about the traffic. I could tell he was trying to keep his annoyance to himself, but something about the drive irritated him to no end.

Since I didn't drive and knew very little about it, I didn't understand why Boston traffic irritated so many people, but at the time, I had no other frame of reference. All I knew was that everybody hated it with a deep passion bordering on fanatical.

When we arrived and disembarked, I carried the donuts and coffee in for him. Jim then headed into his office. I set the things I'd taken in for him on a front desk at his direction.

That done, I wandered out into the soup kitchen which, at this time of day, was closed. Several of the tables were missing, and there was a pale area on the tile near the door where I had sat after being shot as though someone had scrubbed it within an inch of its life. I also saw several holes in the back wall from errant bullets. It felt surreal, and I had to sit down as dizziness overwhelmed me. Everything that had happened over the last two days poured through my head like scenes from a movie. Every movement, every heartbeat, every breath. It took all the air out of me.

Somewhere in the back of my head, I heard Eirlas's voice telling me to count out things I could see, touch, and smell. I took some time to calm myself down, glad he'd taught me how to do that. It didn't solve everything, but the screaming edge of panic died down enough for me to get air into my lungs.

In that moment, that point between panic and understanding, I realized what was wrong in that woman's eyes. What had been in the air. What I'd felt.

It had been demonic in origin.

CHAPTER 18

I peeled my gaze from the floor and let out a shaking sigh. It still felt overwhelming being here, but at least I'd stopped shaking. The whole thing bothered me more than I wanted to admit to—after all, I had faced down literal hordes of demons and defeated them. Two humans with weapons should have been nothing.

The side of my head throbbed a little, and I resisted the urge to touch it, knowing that wouldn't help any and would likely hurt more. Instead, I paced, trying to put together the pieces of the night before. If the two had been influenced by demons somehow, I needed to know why. What had drawn them here? Was it me? If so, I couldn't stay and put all these people at risk.

Poor Mary Beth must have been terrified. The thought made me frown, and I looked toward the door to the shelter's bunk rooms. While Jim had told me nobody had been seriously hurt except me, I still worried. That girl had been through enough. It was still early—only about seven thirty—and the shelter didn't let people in until eight, but I had nothing better to do and headed toward the bunk rooms. I knew Mary Beth wasn't in there, but Eirlas might be doing some cleaning.

The door from the soup kitchen to the bunk rooms led into a hallway with two doors on either side and the bathrooms all the way down at the end. The two rooms, separated by gender, had ten bunkbeds in each, lined up in neat rows with a bank of lockers against a wall allowing for storage of personal items. I had helped Eirlas make beds and do general janitorial work in here. It was also where I had showered when I'd lived at the church.

Eirlas was, as I'd hoped, in the men's bunk room, fussing with a lock on one of the supply closet doors. He had a set of tools in his hands and was muttering, "Of course you forgot your keys. Why wouldn't you forget your keys? You only left them on the table on top of your wallet."

As I watched, he fidgeted with the tools, and the lock popped open, allowing him to open the door. My brows lifted, but the staples in my scalp pulled with the motion, reminding me of their presence. The pain died down with every passing minute, though, and other than my anxiety attack in the cafeteria, I was feeling steadier on my feet.

Eirlas tugged the door open and glanced over his shoulder, pausing. "Cassiel! I hadn't expected you here today after everything that happened. Are you all right?"

"I will heal." I nodded and tried to smile, but it felt a little weak. "I was hoping you knew what became of Mary Beth after what happened. Also, how did you open that door without a key?"

Eirlas's smile faltered. "She hasn't been back. It could be that her father's back in town, but..." He trailed off and shook his head. "I'm just hoping she's all right. She was pretty shaken up—as were the rest of us. Many of our regulars haven't been in since it happened, but I imagine they'll be back soon. And as far as the door goes, I... uh... know a thing or two about getting into places without keys." He didn't seem to want to explain further and pocketed the sleeve of tools.

"Do you know how to find out where her father lives?"

"I have her address on file, but I'm not supposed to share it with her being a minor and all." Eirlas sighed deeply. "But I can't pretend I'm not worried, too. She's still young and in a pretty fragile place." He considered for a moment before a sly smile crept across his features. "Would you like to go for a walk with me? If... if you're up for it." His gaze rested on the healing wound on the side of my head.

I frowned. "That seems an abrupt change of topic. But yes, I am up for it."

"Not at all. I think we could both use some fresh air."

"Jim is going to be looking for me when he finishes with his work."

"So I'll text him and tell him you're with me. It'll be fine. Come." He patted my shoulder and walked past me and out the door.

The feeling that I'd missed something important washed over me as I followed him out of the bunk room and through the church to the outer doors. Eirlas then stepped out and put his hands in his pockets as we walked.

"Where are we going?" I asked as I followed him toward the main throughfare to the west of the church, following the line of the park the church sat near.

"Well, there's a complex near here where a bunch of teenagers live. One of them is a girl. I think you should meet her. Maybe you can help her."

Perhaps he was trying some sort of ruse? Then it clicked. He couldn't tell me where Mary Beth lived because she was still a child. But if he walked with me past the place and did not tell me where she lived directly... I suspected subverting the intent of the law by obeying the letter would not protect him, but if it was what he needed to sleep well at night, I would not argue. Besides, I meant her no harm, and he knew that, I was certain.

"All right, I will meet this girl you know." I walked with him. "I have a question."

"Shoot."

"Why do elves not like the tusked?"

Eirlas grunted. "That's a complicated question, Cassiel. I like tusked folk just fine. Dust's a good friend to me. But... you know elves live a long time, right?"

"Yes. Hundreds of years or longer."

"Right. Has anyone ever talked to you about history? Like, world history."

"Not really. It is not something I have studied."

"Right, well, back in the 1940s, there was this thing called World War II. I'm not going to get into all of it because we could spend months on the subject. It was complicated. But to try and boil it down to the most simplistic terms—it started in Germany and was full of people who believed that all the non-human races, with the exception of elves, were inferior. And even among the humans, there were superior peoples. Mostly those who looked like elves. This one man, Hitler, more or less set wheels in motion to kill millions of people. By the time it ended, most of the world was caught in the conflict, having declared themselves for one side or another.

"In the end, the worst-hit people were the Jews, Romani, homosexuals, Polish, and the tusked races. They lost a lot of people then. With elves living such long lives, there are a lot of us who remember those days and were even part of it. And the tension between elves and tusked never really went away as a result. There are an unfortunate number of elves who still think of the tusked as lesser, and it's a pretty common sentiment in the world. They're seen as big, dumb brutes who aren't worth much, which is a tragedy. They have rich cultures and are just as smart, and stupid, as everyone else. You've met Dust. He's a brilliant chef and a deeper thinker than most people would give him credit for."

As I listened to Eirlas' explanation, my stomach tightened, and I felt somewhat sick. I knew, of course, that humans had waged war on each other many times through the millennia. There were many such references in the numerous holy texts with which I was familiar, but I never really paid attention to the scope of lives lost. Millions of people? I looked around, trying to imagine such a thing. The church, on a packed Sunday, held about a hundred people. I tried to pan that out, multiplying it in my head over and over.

I felt sick. "I need a moment," I said pausing to sit down on the curb, swallowing hard against the lump in my throat.

Eirlas frowned but paused his walk. "I didn't realize history was a difficult subject for you."

"It is not that. It is... Millions of lives lost over something so senseless as that? I cannot even imagine what kind of senseless cruelty it must take for that to happen. How could you let it?"

"I wasn't alive back then, so I didn't. But a lot of people just got taken in by it. You know? They were scared, and when people are scared, a lot of the time, they do stupid things. Like I said, it would take a long time to explain how World War II came about and would mean I'd have to explain World War I. Which is more than we have time for right now. But... ultimately, it boils down to fear."

"But why? What is there to fear from other people? That is what I do not understand."

"These are important questions, Cass, but right now, we have something more immediate to work on. You and I can talk about history later if you want, but I'll be the first to tell you I'm not an expert on it. I just know what I learned in school." Eirlas squeezed my shoulder. "Why don't we focus on the now."

I cleared my throat and took a deep breath. He was right. I could do nothing about something that had happened decades ago, and losing myself in my reaction to it wouldn't help Mary Beth. Nor would it help any of the people who had died back then. It didn't make me feel any better about it, but centering myself in what needed to be done more immediately gave me the strength to stand up and brush myself off. "You are right."

Eirlas patted my back firmly. "It's not far from here."

We walked a little longer, winding north through the maze of streets around the park before we stopped outside a three-story building that I guessed held several apartments, judging by the balconies. "Second floor, 2B," Eirlas said quietly. "I've been here before—I had to talk to her father and get permission for her to stay at the church in writing from him. It was a whole mess. I don't suggest barging up there this minute since Jim's going to be waiting for you, but at least you know where it is now."

I nodded, burning the details into my mind and taking note of the address and street name. Eirlas had been right—it wasn't far from the church at all. "When would be a good time, do you think?" I asked.

"Whenever. Just be careful, Cass. This is kind of a rough neighborhood."

"That does not bother me."

"Maybe, but if you get more messed up, it'll put a dent in your ability to help." Eirlas walked down the street past the apartment and then took a winding route back to the park as though we really were just on a walk. I had enough on my mind that I didn't have much to say on the way back, however.

CHAPTER 19

When we arrived back at the church, Eirlas had me help him with the last of the cleaning both because he'd taken time to walk with me, which left him less to get his work done, and because it gave me something to do while I waited for Jim. Eirlas seemed content to be quiet and just let me work, which was nice. He, Jim, and Dust all appeared to understand my preference for quiet much of the time, and their respectful presence was more of a balm than a hindrance.

I helped him sweep the floors, then took the old sheets into the laundry room adjacent to the kitchen and got the sheets and such going. We washed them with special detergents to kill any parasites that might come in with those who frequented the shelter to both prevent outbreaks at the church and help people avoid spreading them to each other. The people who came there were miserable enough as it was without fleas and bed bugs. We also wiped down the plastic-covered mattresses daily to make doubly certain nothing got established.

The familiar actions felt good, and I was able to sink into them, quieting the storm that had been gathering in my head since the attack. Well, moreover since Father John's death, but it had grown louder since the attack on the church. For a while, at least, there was nothing in my world but cleaning, and when Jim found me, I was folding sheets as they came out of one of the industrial dryers.

"Need a hand?" he asked, nodding to my half-full basket of laundry.

I jumped a little and looked in his direction but nodded. "Oh, if you would like to, I would not turn you down." I smiled a little. He rolled over, and together, we made short work of the remainder of the bedding, folding it and returning it to the basket so it could be stored. "I have something to do this afternoon, if that is all right."

"Ah, sure. I'm not your mom—you can do things without asking. What's up?"

"I wished to check on Mary Beth. Eirlas said she has not come back since the attack, and I wanted to see if she was okay."

"You know where to find her?" Jim raised a brow.

"I have a place I can start, anyway. It may not be where she is, but I am going to look." I picked up the basket of bedding, and Jim and I left the laundry room. He accompanied me while I put it away. I am terrible at lying, so I was grateful that Jim didn't ask how I knew where to find her.

Jim held the basket for me while I put the sheets in the linen closet in the shelter. "Well, if you decide you need help, I can probably give you a hand."

I shook my head. "No, I should be all right." I didn't want to tell him the place wasn't in the slightest bit accessible.

A grunt left him, then he paused, frowning. "I was going to tell you to call me if you need help, but you don't have a phone, do you."

"No." Father John hadn't seen a need to get me one since I stayed at the church, and the church had phones there.

"That's something we can change. It won't be anything fancy, and you won't have a lot of time to talk on it, but it'll work for emergencies." He handed me the empty basket to put in the closet, and I stored it in its place before closing the door and locking it. Despite Father Demoyne disallowing me from staying at the church, I still had my keys. It felt like a stupid thing to assign meaning to, but they had little pieces of tape on them with Father John's writing.

Jim rolled down the hallway with me. "Before you go running off, let's get the phone situation solved. Then you can go do whatever you need to."

"All right."

Jim took me to a corner store and bought me an inexpensive pay-as-you-go phone and programmed the numbers for him, Dust, and

Eirlas into it. He then showed me how to call him and had me try a couple times. It didn't take me long to figure out. I had already known how to use a phone to call 911 in the event of an emergency—Father John had taught me that much using the parish phones. Despite it being a rather small thing, the ability to reach out to the people I relied on felt good, and some of the anxiety of leaving familiar places lessened. While the city was huge, and I could definitely get lost in it, having the ability to contact them meant that if I did lose my way, it wouldn't be forever. Following that, he insisted on having lunch before we went back to St. Mary's.

We arrived back at the church around one. "All right, I'll hang around here for a while and find something to do. You call me if you need me to pick you up, and we can meet back here at, say, six? Then we can get food and head home. Also, how's your head feeling? Your color's better."

That gave me more than enough time, I hoped. If Mary Beth wasn't at her home, I didn't have the faintest idea where to find her, so five hours would either end with me having found her and talked to her or... I didn't want to consider the alternative. "My head is healing. It hurts, but far less than it did this morning. I will be here at six." I nodded. "Thank you, Jim."

He waved a hand. "You've got to do you, Cass. I'm just trying to make sure you're safe while you do." Jim started the process of disembarking as I climbed out of the van, putting my new flip phone in my pocket.

Walking around the van, I waited for Jim to get situated. "Do you need anything before I go?"

"Nah. Go find the girl. Remember—back here at six. Or call me if you're lost or something." Jim pointed at me with a stern expression.

"I will." I smiled and started to re-trace the path Eirlas had taken me on.

The afternoon sun had chased off the early morning chill. Some of the leaves were beginning to change color. It was warm enough today that I could get by in the tee shirt and jeans I wore, but I knew soon I would want to wear warmer clothing. I didn't have much for that, but I had some. If I did laundry often, it was enough.

I shoved my hands in my pockets and fidgeted with the umbrella I kept in my front right one, rolling it over in my fingers. Could Father John's death be connected to the attack on his family years ago? Or was it something unrelated? There were so many unanswered questions. The tactician in me screamed out for data points and intelligence, but I didn't know how to get any of it.

Instead, I focused on making my way to Mary Beth's house. Alone, the streets felt more menacing somehow. I couldn't quite put my finger on it, but even in the brightness of the early afternoon light, I felt as though something lurked around every corner despite nobody appearing to so much as notice me. People walked down the road with their heads low, focused on their own thoughts and problems; others talked loudly into cell phones in languages I didn't recognize or about topics I didn't understand. But most just focused on their own lives and own business.

The neighborhood itself looked like any other street, but that lingering feeling of something *wrong* chased me down the road. I stopped at the building Eirlas had shown me and stared at the window for a moment before walking up the wooden steps to the front door. It, like many Boston buildings in the area, looked quite old and run down. The three-floor structure had cramped balconies on either side, several of which housed decorations for holidays long past or furniture that had been weathered by the sun until the original colors were unrecognizable.

The lock on the front door looked like it had broken some time ago, and I pushed it open with no resistance. Inside, the stairwell zigzagged upwards, sagging a little under the weight of its own existence. Mailboxes hung on the wall to my right, showing six apartments, two per floor if I had to guess. The walls had been painted white some time ago, but many years of what I assumed was neglect had turned them to a dull yellow. The air smelled like cigarettes and rancid cooking oil, and the combination made me grimace.

Orienting myself, I climbed the stairs and looked to the left of the landing where the door sat. This *was* the right apartment, right? A moment of uncertain anxiety washed over me, and I hesitated before straightening my shoulders. No, it had to be the right place. If it weren't, I'd just apologize and look elsewhere. Or double-check with Eirlas that I hadn't made an error.

I drew in a breath and knocked on the door firmly.

Someone moved around inside, shuffling about and something clattered, but whoever it was didn't answer the door immediately. I waited so long, I wondered if maybe they'd chosen not to answer, but an elven man with the same brown hair and green eyes Mary Beth had yanked the door open. "What?"

His sharp manner gave me pause, and I frowned. "Ah… I am a friend of Mary Beth's. I was hoping to see her."

The man gave me a once-over and snorted, his lip curling up in an ugly expression. As attractive as elves were as a race, this man carried none of the grace or appeal inherent in so many of them. In fact, he looked more like a weasel or a rat. His sallow skin hung from his face like a suit several sizes too large for his body. "She doesn't live here no more."

He went to close the door, and I reached out, stopping him. "Where does she live then, sir?"

"I don't fucking know. Don't fucking care, neither." The elf leaned into the doorjamb, attempting to slam the door in my face and failing since I had far more strength in one arm than he did in his entire body, and I had better leverage.

The way he talked about his daughter, with such contempt and disinterest, caused my long-standing frustration and dislike of the man to boil over into something stronger. "She is your daughter, and she might be in trouble. Please. This is important." I did my best to keep my tone even and calm, but some of my outrage must have shown on my face.

Mary Beth's father cowered, retreating backwards into the apartment like an insect, and I pushed the door open again and stepped in. "She's… uh… she's gone." He stepped on a beer bottle on the floor and fell backwards, scuttling away from me like I was going to hurt him.

And, God help me, he wasn't wrong.

CHAPTER 20

What do you mean she's gone?" I shut the door behind me as I closed the distance between us. He had trapped himself up against the shabby remains of a couch that had probably been hideous when it was new and now looked like the seventies had vomited it up after a night of hard drinking.

"Are you fucking deaf?"

"No."

My answer seemed to unsettle him, and his mouth opened and closed a few times. "I'm a businessman. Sometimes, you gotta make deals to get by." He lowered his head, and his lank, greasy hair fell into his face.

The outrage turned into something else. Something harder. I leaned down and grabbed the front of his shirt in my fist, picking him up off the floor and holding him at eye level. "What did you do?" I spat each of the words, my face so close to his I could smell the stink of his breath.

While I don't usually spend much time or effort trying to frighten people, there is a very good reason why one of the first things angels say to a mortal being when we reveal ourselves is, "Be not afraid." Even in a more human guise and lacking the full force of my Grace, I'm capable of being quite intimidating—or so I have repeatedly been told—and this tiny, frail little insect of a man received the full force of my displeasure.

I watched his Adam's apple bob as he swallowed and sweat broke out across his skin. "Who the fuck are you?"

My lips peeled back from my teeth in feral response. "Someone who cares very much about Mary Beth." I didn't know the girl well, but whatever this bastard had done was not what she deserved. And she was a child, for God's sake. *His* child. I hurled him back onto the couch and leaned down over him, one hand on the arm of the couch and the other on the back of it. "Do not make me ask again."

"Fuck off, whoever you are. Whatever you are. She's my kid. My property. S'none of your business." He cringed a little as he said the words and spat at me, trying desperately to hang onto whatever illusions of bravado he'd created around himself.

His head snapped to the side when the flat of my left hand connected with the side of his face. It didn't feel particularly hard to me, but my understanding of my own strength was poor at the time. A welt rose almost immediately and started to bruise under the skin, and he began to sob and blubber. Drool mixed with blood from a split lip poured from his mouth along with the words.

"I g-got in deep with these guys. Owe 'em a lot of money. I've been running product for 'em, and they found out I've been t-taking the edge off now and then." He fumbled a baggie out of his pocket, revealing a couple of tablets. I yanked it from his grip, and he flinched. Somehow, seeing the evidence of what he'd done, holding it in my hand, filled me with rage I couldn't quite understand.

"When I d-didn't pay up, they told me I had to come up with the money somehow. And... elves sell for a lot on—" He stopped talking as my hand closed around his throat, choking off the words.

Every instinct under my skin told me to crush his windpipe. That he was better off facing the Father's judgement. That letting him live would only endanger others. I'd never experienced anger like this and had no idea what to do with it. Not really. It took me a long time to decide to release my grip on him. He couldn't tell me how to find her if he was dead. "Who has her?"

"The BHK!" He gasped. "They have her, okay? Fuck!"

I had no idea who the BHK was, but I knew I needed to walk away before I did something I would later regret. Well, regret more. I let the man go and left the apartment with the little bag of what I assumed was drugs stuffed into my pocket alongside the umbrella. As I stomped down the stairs and out onto the street, I swallowed hard. I didn't know who this BHK was, but I knew Mary Beth was in trouble, and I couldn't fail her like I had Father John.

Putting distance between myself and the apartment building, I headed back toward St. Mary's. Part of me felt sick. Like I couldn't believe I'd struck him. More of me thought he'd deserved it after what he'd done to that poor girl. I didn't understand the full ramifications of it, but I understood enough of the world through the Word that I knew what slavery meant, and in no time on Earth has it ever been good for the person in bondage. As the rush of adrenaline ebbed, my hands began to tremble.

My head spun as I walked. It was well before the six o'clock meeting time I'd arranged with Jim. In fact, my new phone told me it was barely three. It took me about fifteen minutes to make my way back to the church, though instead of heading into the complex, I sat on the bleachers adjacent the baseball diamond occupying the end of the street near the church. I rested my elbows on my knees and my head in my hands.

Her father, her own *father,* had sold her to people because he owed them money. I didn't even know that was a thing that happened in this place. Slavery was long since outlawed, and in my ignorance, I failed to understand that just because it was illegal and invisible didn't mean it didn't happen.

Reaching into my pocket, I pulled out the tablets and scrutinized them. They were small, about the size of the fingernail on my pinkie finger, and colored deep red. A crude image of a knife had been pressed into them when they'd been manufactured. What that meant, I had no idea, but I turned the little bag over in my hands, studying them.

With my mind clearer than it had been back in the apartment, I picked up the faintest trace of energy. Like a scent that vanished if you lingered on it too long. It felt the same as the sense that had come off the people who had attacked the church. I frowned deeply and shook myself, concentrating. Now that I was looking for it, the sense was unmistakable. These definitely felt like the demonic taint those people had. And very similar to the demon I had seen outside Jim's apartment. But what was the connection?

Drugs were, of course, a logical place for demons to focus their efforts. An altered mind would be easier to infiltrate and control. But why attack St. Mary's? Why stalk me directly? I had nothing to do with any of this, and neither had Father John, to my knowledge. Despite having more information, I still felt like I was missing something important. And none of that brought me any closer to finding Mary Beth or knowing who or what this BHK thing was.

I sighed, looking toward the church. While I didn't want to bother Jim if he was busy, I didn't want to wait, either. The longer I did, the harder it would be to find her, and I didn't know exactly when she'd been sold, only that it had been in the last couple days. With that in my mind, I stood and made my way toward the church. Jim would know what to do. He'd known how to handle almost everything so far. This, I told myself, would be no different.

CHAPTER 21

I headed into St. Mary's with a cold, hard feeling in the pit of my stomach. The offices were near the entrance, and I walked into Jim's without knocking. He didn't look up immediately from where he sat hunched over something at his computer, squinting at the screen.

Sinking down into one of the two chairs across his desk from him, I fidgeted a little as I waited. When he finally turned his attention to me, the frown was immediate.

"You okay?"

I shook my head. "No. I am not okay. I am nothing resembling okay." The words came out harsher than I intended. "Her own father sold her. *Sold her*. For these!" I hurled the little zippered plastic bag onto his desk.

Jim closed his eyes and took a long, slow breath. "Tell me everything."

So I did. I told him about the drugs, BHK, and everything Mary Beth's idiot father had said to me. I also told him I'd struck the man, though he didn't seem particularly bothered by the revelation.

"This is way outside my realm of expertise," he said when I'd finished. "Normally, I'd say we should go to the police, but frankly, I'm not sure there's time. And with this being part of the whole... demon situation, I'm not sure it would help. There's one person I can think of who would know enough to help, but he's not going to like this." Jim laced his fingers behind his head and sat back, staring at the ceiling.

"Who?" I frowned.

"Eirlas."

My brows lifted. I knew Eirlas had a drug problem before he started working at St. Mary's, but the idea that he'd know anything about gangs somehow surprised me. "Should I get him?"

Jim nodded. "Let's bring him and Dust in here. We should talk."

I checked my phone's clock again. This time of day, Dust would be just arriving to start prep cooking for tonight's service. I knew where to find him and Eirlas. Their schedules were the same most days with small variations.

Part of me wanted to talk to Jim about how I was feeling. The anger, the faint guilty twinge when I thought about striking that man, but this wasn't the time. We had other things that had to come first. Namely, finding Mary Beth.

I stood up and left the office, heading to the kitchen where I told Dust that Jim needed to talk to him. I then did the same with Eirlas. Both men joined us promptly, though Jim's rather small office felt cramped the moment Dust's broad frame joined us and closed the door behind him.

"Gentlemen," Jim said with a nod. "We have a problem." He laid out what I'd told him, omitting the fact that I'd hit anyone. Dust let out a low, growling noise, and Eirlas's face went pale, and his jaw clenched.

"So," Jim concluded, steepling his fingers with his elbows on the arms of his wheelchair, "obviously, we need to act quickly. We all know how busy the BPD is, and how unlikely it is that they're going to take a seventeen-year-old runaway seriously, no matter what we say. So my guess is, it's up to us. Eirlas, I'm sorry to ask this of you. I know you left that world behind, but—"

Eirlas held up his hands. "No. There are more important things than me avoiding my past. I get that. And I'm not going to hide from this."

Dust grunted and put a hand on Eirlas's back in a comforting gesture. "Not sure what you think I can do to help. I'm just a cook."

Jim's mouth curled up in one corner. "You underestimate yourself. But if nothing else, you can look intimidating as hell and act as muscle if we need it."

"We'll need it." Eirlas crossed his arms in an almost defensive way, looking at the floor. "I know who BHK is, and the only way we're getting anywhere with them is if we look as frightening as possible. If we're lucky, we won't have to back it up, but appearance is everything to these people."

I grunted. "If we need to fight, I can do that."

Dust sighed and shook his head. "I can, but I'd rather not. Just reinforces the stereotype. Gonna do what I can to stay out of that. Though if we have to, we have to. I'm not going to run from it, either."

Jim looked upward, either thinking or praying—I wasn't sure which. But he said nothing for a while. "What can you tell me about the BHK, Eirlas?"

It turned out that BHK stood for "Blue Hill Killaz." The name is stupid, but the organization who claims it is one of the nastier street gangs in Boston. They had started out, as the name suggested, in the neighborhoods around Blue Hill Avenue in Mattapan, but their influence has spread to most of Boston. They are responsible for a good percentage of the drugs coming into and out of the city, and apparently have their fingers in human trafficking as well. However, drugs are their primary focus and source of income.

Eirlas laid out all the information in an emotionless tone, his eyes a little distant. He rubbed at his forearm in an unconscious gesture until Dust put his hand on Eirlas's and squeezed. He didn't say anything, but Eirlas stopped the motion.

"I wasn't in with the BHK, but I knew people who were. Maybe still are. I can maybe arrange a meeting." He swallowed hard, his face set in resolute lines despite his body language telling the rest of us in the room that he wanted nothing to do with any of this. "I can't guarantee we'll find anything or be able to help her, but I can at least get us a foot in the door."

"Better than nothing," Dust said quietly, his hand resting on Eirlas's much smaller shoulder. While displays of affection were very much not in Dust's usual repertoire, he seemed to sense that Eirlas needed the support.

I leaned into the wall and crossed my arms. "How long will this take? She's been gone a couple days by now, and every minute makes it less likely we will find her." It didn't take an expert on missing persons to understand how quickly a trail could go cold.

"Probably until tomorrow. I'll send out a few texts and see what I can rustle up." Eirlas rubbed his hands together in a nervous gesture. "Uh, I've got to finish prepping things for tonight. I'll get the texts sent, but we can't do anything until they reply. And the shelter's still open tonight."

Jim sighed but nodded. "I understand. We'll wait on your word."

"Hey, Eirlas. I've got nothing going on tonight. After dinner, let's chill at my place, huh? I think we could both use the company," Dust said, patting Eirlas's back as they walked out into the hallway, leaving Jim and me alone in Jim's office.

Jim sighed heavily. "This all just got complicated."

"It gets worse," I said when the other two were out of earshot. "Those," I said, pointing to the little baggie on Jim's desk, "have demonic taint on them. And I saw a demon outside your apartment the first night I stayed with you. Whatever's going on here I think ties into why Father John was killed."

"God in Heaven," Jim said, burying his face in his hands. "As if this weren't bad enough already. This stuff," he scoffed, flicking the bag, "is Ripper. It's been everywhere lately. Those two people who came in here and took shots at the..." He trailed off, looking at the side of my head where the bullet wound was still healing. "You don't think there's a connection, do you? Between what happened and Mary Beth and..."

"I do not know. If there is one, I do not understand it yet. But that does not mean it is not there." I sighed and sunk down into the chair at Jim's desk. "I feel like I am trying to put together a puzzle, but I am missing half the pieces and have no idea what the image is supposed to be."

"You and me both." Jim shook his head. "You and me both."

CHAPTER 22

Jim and I went back to his apartment that evening. Neither of us really had a great deal to say, and both of us were too wrapped up in our own thoughts to want to talk much. Jim ordered Chinese food for dinner, and we ate mostly in silence or talked a bit about whether we liked the sauce or not.

After dinner, we settled in to watch the news as Jim seemed to like to do. I sat with him, restless and uncertain. It took me awhile to speak up, but I eventually gathered the courage. "Jim, was I wrong to hit that man?"

He muted the TV and turned toward me. "You're wanting me to tell you it was wrong?"

I couldn't read his expression and shrugged. "I do not know."

"I'm going to have to disappoint you. If I was in your shoes, I'd have done more than slap him. He'd be missing some teeth." Jim grunted and shook his head. "No, Cass. I don't think you did something wrong."

I picked at some dry skin near one of my nails for a moment before answering. "Are we not supposed to forgive?"

"You're more or less human now, right? After your fall?"

The question caught me off guard. "I think so?"

"You don't have to be perfect. But even if you did, don't forget that Jesus beat the money changers out of the temple. Anger isn't a bad thing. The guy's a monster. It's when you let anger get the best of you that it becomes a problem. And, frankly... we both know you could have done much worse. It wouldn't be difficult for you.

"As someone who's done some things he's not proud of in his life, I don't think you did the wrong thing. There are times in the heat of a moment where we have to deal with emotions in ways we aren't prepared for. We're only human. If it's weighing on you, then you should pray on it. Spend some time talking to Him. Ask for forgiveness and guidance."

I nodded, looking at the floor. "I have. And I will. I just wanted to make sure I was not slipping."

"You will slip. You'll fall. You'll make mistakes. You'll sin and do things you regret. You're human, Cass. We all make mistakes. The only thing for it is to try and focus on doing the right thing and learn. We don't really have other options."

He was right, and I knew it. But I still worried. I nodded in response to his words, and when I didn't say anything else for a while, Jim unmuted the TV, letting me mull over what he'd said.

Jim tapped out and went to bed around nine, leaving me the remote with the understanding that I could watch TV if I felt the inclination. I didn't, but it was a kind gesture anyway.

Instead, I lay on the couch, staring at the ceiling, worrying about what the next day would bring.

Eirlas texted Jim around seven in the morning, just as I was getting out of the shower, and he was eating breakfast. I heard his phone go off where he was holding it, scrolling through an article of some kind. He tapped at the screen and nodded. "Got a meeting at ten."

"So soon?" My brows rose. I hadn't expected it to happen that quickly, though I was anything but ungrateful. "I did not think they would want to talk to us at all, let alone immediately."

"There's some stuff you don't know about Eirlas, Cass. He wasn't just a drug addict—he was a dealer, and he was one of the upper guys in a group not too unlike BHK."

My jaw almost hit the table as I thought about it. Eirlas? He was so gentle and worked so hard to take care of everyone who walked into the shelter. I had a hard time picturing him dealing drugs or doing any of the things I had been led to believe such people did. "Did he... did he do things like what is happening to Mary Beth?"

Jim shook his head and waved his spoon over his cereal bowl for punctuation. "No. He had nothing to do with anything like that. Ever. When he first came to the shelter after he got out of prison, we vetted him pretty hard. He's not that kind of guy."

I settled down a little, relieved that I hadn't been wrong about Eirlas's nature. "Good." I finished drying my hair and put my towel on the rack to dry before joining him in the kitchen. I didn't feel hungry, but I poured myself some cereal anyway, knowing Jim would scold me if I didn't eat. And I needed to be fully focused on the meeting, not hungry and distracted.

"People change over time. It's one of the few things we can rely on in the world," Jim said. "The Bible talks a lot about repentance and the power of deciding to let go of what you used to be. Eirlas is no different."

I sighed and nodded. He was right, of course. But after what I'd seen and learned, I found it difficult to swallow the idea that Eirlas had run with the sorts of people who would engage in such things, even if he, himself, had no contact with it. I resolved to talk to him about the whole thing when we were under less immediate pressure. Now wasn't the time to be cutting out friends, though part of me wondered if he and I could be that anymore. How many people had he hurt? Had he indirectly killed? I wrestled with that in silence, trying to come to terms with who Eirlas was now versus who he had been.

After we finished eating, Jim looked at the staples along the side of my head and told me they were ready to remove. Much like he did at church, he had an impressive med kit that he kept under his bed, and he made short work of the staples. While the holes where the staples had been remained, and I had no hair over the place the gash had been, it hadn't scarred. The wounds Arazael had left me were different, confirming my theory that it was a reminder of my failure.

Jim and I arrived at the unremarkable building in Mattapan shortly before ten. Most of the buildings on the street looked more or less the same: three stories, obviously housing several apartments, and varying shades of blue, gray, or taupe. They had a similar look to most of the other architecture I'd seen in this area of the city, which I later learned was considered the New England style.

Eirlas met us on the sidewalk with an uneasy smile. "So, ah, listen. You should let me do most of the talking here, all right? These guys don't know you, and they're kind of... Well, you'll see." He stuffed his hands in his pockets, shoulders hunched a little as he stared at the concrete. "They might not know much about what you're looking for, but it's worth a shot. They'll at least know more than the police, anyway."

He looked tired. Dark circles stained his pale skin, and it didn't look like he'd showered yet. While I'd seem him tired before, this sort of weariness didn't quite seem like it made sense. Maybe he hadn't slept? When I gave him a once-over, I realized he was wearing the same clothes he had been the day before. Just how late had he been out with Dust?

I nodded once, and Jim echoed the gesture. "Thank you," I offered, trying to force a smile.

It must not have looked genuine because Eirlas looked away. "Yeah. Anything I can do to help Mary Beth."

Jim studied the building and shook his head. "I'm going to wait in the car."

I opened my mouth to ask him not to when I realized the problem: stairs. While I could've picked him up—chair and all—and lifted him up the front set of stairs, if there was no ramp here, I doubted there would be easy access inside.

Eirlas frowned. "Oh, uh... shit. Sorry, Jim. I should've thought—"

Jim cut him off with a wave of his hand. "You've had enough on your mind with this meeting. Data's more important. You'n Cass head in. I'll get us some coffee." Frustration washed across Jim's features, but he pulled himself straighter in his chair. "This is more important than me. Go on." He gestured to us with a "shoo" motion.

No part of me wanted to be alone with Eirlas at that moment, or alone with those other people, and the rage that had swam up from the pit of me the day before hovered in the periphery, threatening to swamp me. I grit my teeth and took a slow breath while telling myself I didn't have a choice.

Eirlas glanced at me and jerked his head toward the door. "C'mon. Let's get this over with." He then headed inside. I walked in after him into the stairwell. "I should've thought about Jim," he said with a sigh, running a hand over his greasy hair. "But they probably wouldn't want to talk about this anywhere else."

I shrugged. "We all have a lot on our minds right now." I kept the words as mild as I could and looked around. The place smelled vaguely of some kind of urine mixed with an odd, pungent, herby scent I couldn't identify.

Eirlas glanced at me but didn't answer, leading me up to the third floor where he knocked on the door and opened it to let us inside.

CHAPTER 23

I don't know what I'd expected, really, but it wasn't what I saw. The door opened into a cramped kitchen with cracked, peeling linoleum flooring stained yellow with what I could guess was smoke. Dirty dishes filled the sink and overflowed onto the counter, playing host to flies that hovered around them with a low buzz.

It took most of my considerable fortitude to not cover my nose as I entered, but I couldn't stop the way my face screwed up in revulsion. Eirlas didn't seem to notice the mess and walked in, gesturing for me to follow.

Eager to get out of the kitchen, I followed. The living room wasn't much better than the kitchen had been, and I found no relief. Clothes were scattered everywhere in piles, stinking of unwashed bodies. There wasn't much room to walk without stepping on plates covered in molding food, laundry, or other debris scattered around the floor.

Four men hunkered on the couch and a chair in the living room, blank expressions glued to the TV while they played a video game. All were elven, which made the circumstances of their surroundings all the more horrifying in a way. Few creatures could match or eclipse the sheer physical beauty of elvenkind, so to see them in such a state struck me as doubly wrong somehow.

Eirlas flopped down into an empty armchair, far too comfortable in the surroundings. One of the men playing games offered him what looked like some kind of cigarette, and I recognized it as the source of the herby scent I'd smelled earlier. Eirlas shook his head and lifted a hand. "Nah, man. Not this time."

His entire demeanor had changed somehow. I couldn't quite put my finger on it, but it was like looking at a mattress without sheets. Sure, it was technically the same, but sleeping on it still felt wrong.

He spoke slowly. "Guys, this is my friend Cass. I told you about her earlier. Looking for a friend of ours."

One of the men nodded a little and hit "pause" on the game, causing the other three to sulk and glare at him, but he gave them a sharp look. They backed down, and at that moment, I guessed he was the one more or less in charge. "Yeah. You did. Look, man. I'll help how I can, but sticking your nose in BHK business is bad news. Lotta people get dead doing that."

I bit my tongue to stifle me telling them I quite knew how to handle myself, thanks.

"I know. But we gotta try. You know the cops. Won't get their blues dirty helping look for people like us. So we've gotta stick together." Eirlas rested his elbows on his knees and shook his head. "You have any idea where BHK is moving people through?"

Having made no move to introduce me to the guy, I got the hint that I wasn't meant to know who I was talking to. Instead, I shifted my weight a little and crossed my arms, trying to ignore the nauseating stink in the apartment.

The two talked for a minute, discussing addresses and times, but I couldn't understand much of it since they slipped into a language I assumed was elven. Eirlas's contact shot me furtive glances now and then when he thought I wasn't looking, but I didn't look back.

Instead, I let my gaze wander around the room. With nothing else to do, I tried to figure out what the various and sundry items covering the floor were. I recognized hypodermic needles from my time in the hospital. Some kind of tubing. A spoon. A candle. Alcohol bottles of many shapes and sizes. Several magazines I figured were pornography. My nose wrinkled a little at that, and I averted my gaze from those quickly.

One of the men on the couch offered me the same cigarette he'd tried to give to Eirlas, his crooked smile displaying several missing teeth. Even his elven heritage couldn't smooth over the fact that he looked like a withered husk of a person. His cheeks had sunken in, and his skin looked older than I'd seen any elf appear yet. Brittle.

I shook my head. "I do not smoke. It would not do anything for me anyway. But thanks."

He shrugged in a manner that suggested he thought I was missing out on something and took a long, slow drag before passing it off to one of the others. The man then went back to playing video games.

This wasn't my first time around drugs. I'd seen enough use of them in people at the shelter, albeit never done in front of me. Many of the homeless I worked with—we worked with—had struggles with addiction in various forms, though not all of them. My mind went to Mary Beth, and I grit my teeth.

It was tempting to blame all of these people for their own circumstances, but I knew as well as any of them that all it took was one mistake, and an entire life could change. While I had a place to sleep and food to eat, I had spent enough time with those who didn't to understand it.

More than once, I had envied Father John for his ability to find some kind of solace in alcohol. Such things, I knew objectively, weren't good in the long term, but having the option to not be present with everything in my head at all times held a certain appeal to me.

The conversation ended, and Eirlas shook the man's hand before nodding to me and walking out. I followed him into the hallway, and we descended the stairs without comment. I wanted to ask Eirlas what he'd learned but guessed he'd tell Jim and I when we were together. No use in explaining the thing more than once.

I kept my peace as we made our way out to Jim's van, already parked and waiting. He unlocked the doors and handed us each a hot cup of coffee as we climbed in. He also handed us each a small bag.

"I—"

Jim shushed me. "Food first, explanations after." He then fired the van up and drove away from the curb, not waiting for either of us to reply.

Another minute of agonizing silence passed as the two of us ate our bagels (blueberry for Eirlas, cinnamon-raisin for me) and washed them down with the warm coffee.

CHAPTER 24

S o, I don't know everything, but I know a few things. I don't know how much use they'll be, but..." Eirlas let out a trembling sigh.

Jim glanced at him in the rearview mirror. "Eirlas, look at me." He must have because a second later, Jim went on. "You are alive. You are present. You aren't using." His tone was steady and calm.

Silence reigned between them for a minute, but I heard Eirlas draw a deep breath behind me. "Yeah. Thanks." He cleared his throat and continued. "So, turns out Mary Beth's dad is a dealer for BHK. I don't know a lot else, but it makes sense that he had product. From what I understand, the guy's known for... sampling his wares a lot. If you catch my meaning."

I frowned. "I do not."

Jim shook his head. "Think of it this way, Cass. If a baker eats all his cupcakes, he won't have any to sell. Worse, if a drug dealer does the drugs, he won't be able to keep his head straight. So it's extra problematic for them."

My lip curled in an expression of disgust. "Ah."

"My guess is he sold her to cover his debts. Now BHK doesn't do a lot of human trafficking, but most of what they *do* is north of here. Columbus Park, South Boston... From what I understand, they also like to keep girls up there around Static," Eirlas said.

Jim lifted a hand, balled his fingers, and looked like he was going to hit the steering wheel, but he took a few breaths and controlled himself. "She's too young for any of that."

"What is Static?" I asked, trying to understand the response the name had elicited.

"It's a vampire club up that way. He's saying they're likely to pimp her out as a blood doll. Get her hooked on that, and she won't be as likely to try and escape," Eirlas explained, his voice quiet.

"How are we supposed to locate her?" My shoulders tensed, my whole body reacting as though I could somehow punch my way out of the situation. Not that I could, no matter how much I wanted to. "Can we not just tell the police what we know?"

"We can, and... we probably should, but I don't think that'll save her," Jim said. "Eirlas, why don't you come back to my place with us. I figure you should be with friends. That, and I'm going to call Dust and have him come by. We can get all of us updated and figure out what our next move is."

Eirlas nodded, and we returned to silence as Jim drove, the quiet broken only by the sound of Eirlas's phone indicating he had a text.

When we reached Jim's apartment, Dust was waiting on the sidewalk outside, hands stuffed into his pockets. Passersby were giving him side-eye as they passed, but he didn't seem to notice. If he did, he was making specific effort to ignore them.

When we dismounted from the car, Dust nodded to the three of us, and we piled into Jim's apartment and huddled around the kitchen table. There wasn't really enough space for three, let alone for Dust being such a large man, but we managed.

Eirlas laid out what he knew about BHK and about Mary Beth's father and how their businesses operated. The muscles in Dust's jaw clenched while he listened, and his shoulders and upper back coiled like he was ready to strike someone. However, he remained perfectly still. When he finally spoke up, his tone was as dead calm as I'd ever heard despite the obvious fury gathering in him. "So what's the next move?"

Jim leaned back in his chair, arms crossed. He wore a similar mantle of fury and calm to Dust, while Eirlas's gaze darted back and forth between them. The cords of his throat tensed as Eirlas swallowed, and his skin looked a little paler than usual. For all I still couldn't process Eirlas of all people being part of that world, I couldn't ignore his response and reached over to touch his shoulder where he sat beside me, squeezing it. He felt so frail under my larger hand.

"I think we should go about this twofold. First, we tell the police. Second, we start looking. There's something else about this you should know." Jim's gaze slid to me. "It's time you told them."

Both Dust and Eirlas looked at me expectantly, and I lowered my hand from Eirlas's shoulder. "Is now really a good time for this conversation, Jim?" I asked. "I think they may have enough to—"

Dust cut me off with a growl. "Out with it. If we're going to plan a response, we need all the data."

I chewed my lip for a moment, feeling as nervous as Eirlas looked. "Right, so… I am certain you have heard the rumors about me calling myself an angel. I stopped talking about it pretty early on, but you may have heard it, I guess." I stumbled over my words a little.

Eirlas shrugged, and Dust let out a grunt. "Heard about it. Sounded a little stupid."

"Well, it is true. Normally, I would not have brought it up, but this situation with Mary Beth is more than just human trafficking. There are demons involved. My guess is that it is related to the demon that killed Father John."

Dust stared at me for a long time, then looked at Jim. "You buy this shit?"

Jim nodded once.

"Look, Cass. You're a nice person. I like you. But this isn't the time for—"

I sighed. "This is why I did not want to tell them." I stood up and removed my jacket. In my frustration, I wasn't really careful about my environment, and when I called my wings, they snapped open and knocked things over on the counter, sending a glass to the floor. My shirt was one designed for a creature with wings, so it didn't damage the shirt to call them out, thankfully. Both Dust and Eirlas recoiled. Doubly so when I called holy fire to my hands, the tongues of flame licking up my forearms to my elbows and casting stark, white light across the room.

"I am sick of being told I am crazy. I am sick to death. I am what I claim, and while this world may largely be a mystery to me, I am *not* a fool, and I am *not* damaged. I am also *not* lying. Demons are real. Heaven is real. And you attend a church every week worshipping the God who made us all."

I growled a curse in Enochian—insomuch as there *are* curses in Enochian—and ran my hands through my hair. "We do not have time for disbelief and denouncement. There are real demons, and the drug her father is peddling, which he got from the BHK, has demon taint on it. Whatever is happening involves them, which is part of the reason why leaving this affair to the police will not work. If there are demons involved, they will not be capable of handling this themselves. Just like they are not going to find the being that killed Father John."

"Cass!" Jim's tone cut through my frustration, and I looked at him. "If you don't put your wings away, you are going to knock everything over. My apartment isn't big enough for those. You have made your point. Now clean up the glass you broke and sit down." Despite remaining cool, his tone offered no room for argument.

Taking a deep, slow breath, I banished my wings again and adjusted my shirt, dismissing the holy fire and going to where the dustpan and broom were stored before cleaning the mess. My movements were the only sounds in the space as I opened and closed the cabinet. The relative silence just made me all the more aware of every single sound I made.

At the table behind me, I heard Jim clear his throat. "Now that that's clear, you can understand the stakes. We are dealing with something bigger than human trafficking, but whatever this is, Mary Beth is up to her neck in trouble, and we've got to get her out."

Dust spoke up first, his voice trembling a little. "Okay, so there's demons. What makes you think this has anything at all to do with Father John's murder?"

I finished cleaning up the broken glass and threw it away before turning to face them. Eirlas wouldn't look at me and kept his head low. Dust, on the other hand, was looking almost harder than he had before. He seemed a bit paler than usual, but otherwise, he didn't appear to be responding to the revelation. Perhaps it was the soldier in him leading him to think about what came next. I didn't know.

I leaned a hip against the counter and crossed my arms against my chest. "The drugs that snake is peddling carry a demonic taint to them. It's too faint to tell if it's the same demon that is responsible for Father John's murder, but one has been sniffing around since he died. I saw it here a few days ago. While it is possible the events are entirely unrelated, it does not feel like they are to me.

"Before my fall, I stood as a guardian of one of the gates of Heaven. It was my duty to watch for threats and defend against them. It is what I was literally created to do. I do not have immediate proof, just a feeling. But in my experience, there are very few coincidences when it comes to demons."

Dust took a slow breath when I talked about what I did before my fall, but he nodded. Jim spoke up again, taking control of the situation in a smooth, confident manner. "I hadn't intended the revelation to be quite so dramatic as it was, but there we have it. Eirlas, you're looking pretty green. You want some water?"

Wordless, Eirlas nodded.

Rather than having Jim bother with it, I got a glass and filled it, setting it on the table in front of Eirlas before returning to my seat.

Looking between the other three, I asked, "So. Now what?"

CHAPTER 25

O nly things I can think of aren't the kind of tactics we should probably be using here," Dust said, sighing. "I figure you've thought about that already, Jim?"

Jim nodded. "Much as I don't want to consider it, yes."

I raised a brow and looked between them in silent question.

"The way I'd handle this overseas would be to catch a member of the gang and give them good reason to provide information. It's not legal and could be dangerous with it just being the four of us."

"Capture them?" I tilted my head. "What would you need to do that?"

"Place to take them that people wouldn't be wandering through. I don't want to do them serious harm—torture doesn't really work—but there are other ways. Bribery, fear, all sorts of things," Jim answered, looking uncomfortable at the notion. "Sometimes, threats of violence are enough."

"I can be very threatening," I offered.

"Yes, you can, but we need to first find someone who knows something. Which would mean locating someone with some level of authority."

Eirlas drank the entire glass of water in one go. "I remember a few names," he said quietly.

"First, we call the police and tell them what we know. I'll handle that," Jim said. "Eirlas and I are both church workers and know her. We'll let them know we're worried and heard rumors. They can at least get started on their end. They've got resources we don't. And who knows—maybe they'll find her first. If they do, that's one less problem for us."

"I'm confused," Dust said. "One less? Isn't that the whole point of this?"

I shook my head. "Your whole focus is the girl. Once she is safe, then your role in this is finished. My end goal is the demon. Whichever one is behind this, their structure needs to be crushed from the top if we are to drive it out of the city and stop whatever plans it has in motion."

"What would it even want?" Dust asked, frowning and leaning back in the chair, which groaned under his substantial weight.

"Any number of things. Power, of course, being the most likely. I am not even certain what kind of demon it is. Were I to guess, I would think it likely either a demon of rage or a demon of inspiration. As for its goals... I do not know what it wants or why. That is beyond me."

"All right, so our plan is for me to call the police and talk to them about Mary Beth having gone missing. Eirlas, if you remember names, let's see what you can do with your network. Dust, can you maybe find a quiet place to have a conversation with the person Eirlas identifies? We're not looking to do anything terrible, but... just make them think we are." Jim closed his eyes as he spoke, breathing slowly.

Dust nodded. "Can do that. We looking to start this now?"

"The longer we wait, the worse our chances are," Jim answered.

"What is my role in this?" I asked, frowning.

"Looking scary, more or less. We put the fear of God into this person. *Without* hurting them. Clear?"

I grunted. "I will do my best."

"I've got a movie for you to watch. Might give you an idea. Eirlas, Dust, get going. I'm going to introduce Cass to the Punisher."

"Uh, which version?" Dust asked, his brows knitting.

"Thomas Jane."

A smirk appeared on Dust's face. "*Si vis pacem, para bellum.*" He looked at Eirlas, patting his back. "Come on. Let's get out of here. Got work to do." Dust then looked at me for a long moment without saying anything before he left.

Eirlas glanced at me and then away again as he stood and scuttled toward the door.

Alone once again with Jim, I took the glass Eirlas had used to the sink and washed it. "I am sorry for breaking the other glass," I said, not sure what else to say.

Jim shrugged. "Walmart special. I can get another. But you were a little harder on them than necessary, you know. Could've broken it to them more gently."

"I am just so sick of being treated as though there is something wrong with me. As though I am either lying or delusional. I am neither. You would think men of faith would know truth when they see it."

Jim chuckled. "Unless I see the nail marks in his hands and put my finger where the nails were and put my hand into his side, I will not believe."

That gave me pause, and I sighed, leaning both hands on the sink. "You are right. I will apologize." Guilt crawled up my spine. Of course they wouldn't believe. They hadn't believed in the Son until he had shown Himself to them, so expecting them to believe me without proof was unfair, and I knew it. "I have been fighting with my wrath since I found out what happened to Mary Beth. I do not know what to do with it, and it feels like a fire burning out of my control."

I didn't hear him move, but Jim hugged me from behind and a little to the side. "I understand, Cass. This is a lot. I get it. Right now, we need to keep that anger focused where it belongs: on the people who have been hurting others. We can't afford to turn on each other. Honestly, I'm surprised Eirlas didn't faint when you yelled at him like that. People who've never dealt with the divine before don't understand how to process it. It takes time."

"Should I have told them to not be afraid?"

He laughed, and I felt the resonance of it through my side before he pulled away. "You know, I don't think that, at any time in the history of mankind, that has ever once worked."

"Then why do we always say it?"

"I haven't the faintest idea."

Jim had me watch *The Punisher*, focusing on a specific scene and showing how Mister Castle scared but did not hurt the man called Micky using an ice pop and pretending it was, instead, very hot. After the scene ended, I asked, "So the goal here is to encourage this person to tell us what we need to know without doing them harm?"

"Yes." Jim nodded, pausing the DVD.

"But allowing them to think harm is being done to them is acceptable?"

He nodded a second time. "So long as you aren't really hurting them, yes."

"I see. I believe I can manage that." I stopped, a smirk appearing on my face as I turned toward Jim. "I will also not tell him to not fear me."

He burst out laughing. "That's a smart choice, yes." Jim then left me to watch the rest of the movie while he called the police to talk to them about what had happened. Well, part of it, anyway. From what I gleaned of the conversation, he told them Mary Beth hadn't been coming to the church for a few days, and he was worried about her, so he asked them to do something called a "wellness check." It wasn't a long conversation, and he soon returned to the living room.

While my frustration, urgency, and anger had settled into a low simmer, I still felt like I might burst out of my skin at any moment. So when I felt the faint, putrid sensation of demonic taint outside the apartment, I was on my feet and moving before I realized what I was doing. Jim called after me, but I didn't answer.

Instead of merely watching it through the window this time, I left the apartment and stormed out into the mid-afternoon sunlight. I felt the presence a short way down the sidewalk and looked in that direction. A man wearing jeans and a turtle-neck shirt smiled at me from where he leaned against one of the trees, the expression crooked. Human, I realized. Was he possessed? Influenced somehow? I glared at him, not returning the smile.

"So rude, fallen. We are kin, you and I."

"What do you want, and why are you here?" I ignored the attempt to anger me, despite the fact that the idea that he and I were somehow kin made the pit of my stomach clench and roil.

"Cass?" Jim's voice followed me out the door.

"Stay inside!" I barked without looking back at him.

The demon's smile grew, and he looked over my shoulder toward the building. "Such fragile creatures you ally yourself with, fallen. It would be a pity if they came to harm because you were too pigheaded to know when to keep your feathers to yourself, wouldn't it?"

I grunted, trying not to rise to the bait. "Was it you who killed Father John?"

"What is it these humans say…" The man tapped a thin, long finger to his lips in thought for a moment as he looked upward in a manner more exaggerated than genuine. "I plead the fifth."

Not understanding what he meant, I stepped forward, my hands curling into fists at my sides. "Cease speaking in riddles, demon." The anger I had just managed to coax into a simmer burst into full fire in my chest, and it was all I could do not to launch across the distance between us and choke the life from him.

A sigh, and the demon rolled his eyes so hard, I wondered if it would actually injure the host. "How dull you are. Fine. I'd forgotten how literal your kind is sometimes and how little you know of the world. You should lighten up. Get laid, maybe." The demon laced his fingers and put his hands behind his head, pushing off the tree to stand upright. "I'm here because you're starting to get into things I'd rather you didn't, and I am ever so politely asking you to stop."

"You killed my friend."

"Allegedly."

"And you are peddling this… this poison in the city." I pulled the little baggie of pills out of my pocket and shook it in the demon's direction. I didn't know exactly what the word meant, but I could guess, in context, it was a denial.

"Allegedly."

"So no. I will not."

"Tsk. What a shame. Well, you can't say I didn't warn you, fallen. Which is what this is: a warning. Stay out of my way, and I will stay out of yours. If you don't, I cannot promise people you care for will not be hurt. Perhaps even killed."

Jim spoke up from behind me. "*Sancted Michael Archangele, defende nos in proelio…*"

The demon squinted in his direction. "How rude." That said, he backed away as though the words themselves caused him discomfort. His eyes, flicking from the human host's dark brown to glowing red, bored into mine. "I'll be seeing you." Without warning, the demon leaped into traffic in front of a rather large truck.

CHAPTER 26

The truck struck the demon's host, sending him spinning to the side. Slamming on the brakes, the driver narrowly avoided hitting a parked car as the vehicles behind the driver spun and skidded. Without thinking, I shoved the bag in my pocket and rushed forward, slipping between the tons of moving steel and rubber like a bird through clouds. I paid them no heed as cars swerved around me and tires screeched.

Instead, I moved to the collapsed body, dropping down beside it and reaching to touch the bloody mass of flesh and cloth that had once been a man. I felt no pulse. Rage filled me, boiling through my veins and setting my flesh alight as holy fire licked across my skin. My wings snapped open in what was likely a surprising display for those around me.

"No," I snarled, drawing on the shallow pool of Grace available to me. Another innocent would not die to this demon while I stood by helpless to stop it. I couldn't let it happen. I pressed my hand to the man's chest and closed my eyes, feeling for the spark of his soul.

What most people don't know is that everyone has at least a spark of Grace in them. It is, after all, what a soul is—the pure mote of perfect light, the thing of which the universe was crafted. It is the miracle of life that all beings possess. From dandelions to children, all are imbued with a flicker of His touch.

Before my fall, I had been a creature of pure Grace, but in human form, my flesh acted as almost a prison for that power. After all, physical bodies had boundaries that my previous form lacked. Drawing on my Grace as I was, I could feel my flesh splitting and cracking under the strain, but I didn't stop. I joined my Grace to the flickering mote of the dying man's and poured my power into him. I felt it fill in the spaces where he was broken, seeping into his body like water into parched earth.

The tiny, fading glimmer of his soul guttered and then burst to life as I gave him my Grace. While on the outside, it likely looked as though I was merely healing his wounds, I was doing more than that. I was undoing the damage the demon had done to his soul. Where once this would have been effortless, I had to struggle to maintain it now.

Time ceased to have meaning as I worked, but I was vaguely aware of people around me. The howl of sirens. The chatter of voices. A moment later, a pair of hands grabbed my shoulders, drawing me out of my focus, and I whipped my head around. Instantly, I regretted it as the world tilted and spun, my vision going dark.

~

When I woke, I was in Jim's apartment, lying on the couch. Every fiber of my body ached, and my head felt like it had been under the wheels of the truck that had struck the poor man the demon had used as a host. I lifted a hand to touch my head and hissed as it moved, stinging fire flooding up my hand and forearm.

"I don't know what in the hell you were doing, but you did a number on yourself." Jim's voice sounded tense and almost angry.

I frowned and looked at my hand, seeing it swathed in gauze. I then turned my head to locate Jim. He was sitting by the couch in easy reach of me. "You are angry with me?" I asked, frowning, though the motion hurt a little. The room was a bit of a mess, and I noticed blood smeared on the coffee table and on several towels lying around on the floor.

"Angry isn't the right word. Just... I know you don't understand the world well, but using magic to heal someone's illegal. I had to do a lot of explaining to get you out of that, and even then, I think they're suspicious."

"Who?"

"The police, Cass. They showed up after you passed out. You made a hell of a spectacle of yourself. It's a small miracle you weren't charged with something."

"Did he live?" I sat up and groaned as pain shot through me.

"Yes."

"Then it is worth it." I examined the gauze covering my arms and realized it was stained with dried blood. "I hurt."

"No wonder. Your arms look like you tried to stick 'em in a food processor while it was running. I got you out of there before the EMTs tried to drag you off, but if you were anything but what you are, I'd have sent you straight to the hospital."

"I will heal," I answered, shaking my head a little and regretting it. "How long was I out?"

Jim grunted. "Few hours. I heard back from Dust'n Eirlas. Dust has a location, but Eirlas is still trying to decide on our target. But at this point, I'm not sure I want you anywhere near the interrogation."

"Why not?"

"I know you can't see what's going on under those bandages, Cassiel, but you're pretty badly hurt, and I don't want you collapsing. If we're going to have to fight demons, that's more important than scaring the information out of some middle-management fool." Jim shook his head, running his hands through his hair and sighing. "Besides, I'm capable of scaring him. I just don't really like the thought of it. That part of my life is over. Has been for years. Going back there…" He trailed off with a sigh. "I know you heal quickly. I've seen it. But we may not have a day for you to rest."

I knew very little about what Jim had done in the military, only that he had been a Marine and told me he had been something called a "drill instructor." But I knew enough about combat to understand his sentiment about wishing to avoid it. I didn't have the same aversion to it, but perhaps that was due to my nature. It was, after all, what I had been created to do.

"How bad are my arms?"

"I didn't really look. I just wrapped them as quick as I could to get pressure on them. We should clean 'em up, though."

"I cannot get sick. Nor can I get an infection."

"That doesn't mean they won't heal better if they're properly tended," Jim replied and pointed at me. "Besides, it'll make me feel better."

Sighing, I nodded. "If it will make you feel better, I will let you do what you need." When I went to stand up, everything spun a little, and I sunk back down. "I am sorry—I need to stay seated for now."

"It's okay." Jim puttered about, returning with a lap full of medical supplies and a mixing bowl he'd put warm water into. Carefully, he unwrapped my forearms, using water to loosen the gauze where it stuck to the dried blood underneath. The process hurt, but I had endured worse. When he revealed the extent of what I had done to myself, I grunted. Deep splits covered my forearms as though my body had cracked under the strain. I could still use my hands, so it must not have damaged the muscles or tendons, but moving them hurt a good deal nonetheless.

"I've seen casters do things to themselves before, but this is… What happened, Cass?"

"This body was never designed to withstand the use of Grace the way angels use it. It began to break down."

"Grace?"

I explained the nature of Grace and its relation to the soul to him as best I could. The mortal tongues are inadequate to grasp the truth of the matter, but I got as close as I could to it. Jim listened in silence as he worked to clean and re-bandage my forearms.

"So helping that man could have killed you."

"Yes."

"And you were willing to die to save a demon?"

I gave him an annoyed look. "The man was not a demon. A demon had possessed him, but the man was no such creature."

"There any way you can stop a demon from possessing you? I know what the Bible says, but I get the feeling that isn't the whole story." He looked a bit shaken but was holding himself together well.

"Knowing they are now becoming so aggressive, I will pray on the matter. I know there are ways, but the only one I am certain of is not something you, Dust, or Eirlas would likely enjoy."

He finished bandaging and secured the gauze with tape. "Best I can do. Why wouldn't we like it?"

"I would need to brand you with my sigil. It would be quite painful, and I lack the tools to make such a thing. I could bless the three of you instead—it would be better than nothing. Your faith would be a great deterrent to such possession, however. While it will not protect you from all things, it would make the demons far less likely to attempt such a thing."

Jim headed into the kitchen to dispose of the bloodied gauze and wash his hands. "Yeah, that doesn't sound like it's going to be possible at the moment. We'll have to look for a different way. But our faith protects us?"

"Yes, to some extent. Faith is a powerful thing, and true faith provides a great deal more defense than many other methods. The faith doesn't have to be Christian, either. Anyone with pure faith in *something* has some measure of protection." I flexed my hands a little, feeling the bandaging pull and grimacing. Despite healing quickly, I experienced pain as any mortal being did.

"What did it want, anyway?"

"The demon?"

"Yes."

A sigh left me, and I closed my eyes, trying to control the instantaneous anger that thinking of the demon filled me with. "It was warning me off. I was right—it is the same one that killed Father John. We must be getting close to something if it was willing to send so direct a message."

Jim returned to the living room and transferred himself to his recliner, leaning back and staring at the ceiling. "I'm having trouble connecting the dots. The demon's peddling a drug in the city. We blundered into that looking for Mary Beth. I get that part. But what does it have to do with Father John's death? Why him?"

I chewed over the question and sighed. "Demons are focused creatures most of the time. Shrewd. Smart. At least the more powerful ones, anyway. Father John must have gotten in its way somehow. Stepped on its toes. Archdemons like him do not kill without reason, so there has to be a connection."

Jim rubbed at his chin in thought. "You know... there was his 'Clean Sweep' program."

I'd heard Father John talk about it before. For all St. Mary's sits at the heart of one of the city's low-income districts, Father John didn't see it as a place deserving of neglect. He'd been working with a number of other local churches and organizations to start programs to support and maintain the local parks and do things like add flowers around the city-sponsored housing. In addition to that, he had been working with the school nearby to fund after-school programs for the kids who were most at risk. Of course, this was in addition to the clothing donations, soup kitchen, and shelter.

I smiled a little. His charity and endless belief in the good in the people around him had been one of my favorite qualities about him. And he hadn't for a second believed that the people in the streets around the church weren't as good and hardworking as those who had more money. "Everyone needs a hand sometimes, Cass," he'd explained. "Most people are only a disaster away from being right down in the gutter with us, so I'd rather work on picking people up than spend my energy judging 'em for having fallen in the first place."

"That could be it," I said after a long few minutes.

"Yeah. Think about it. He was always working to get people out of those places. The groups at the church, the work he did... there's a lot of things pointing to it. But," a frown crossed Jim's face, and he sat straight up, "does this mean everyone working to make the community safer is at risk?"

The idea sunk into the pit of my stomach like a stone into a pond. "Yes. That is exactly what that means."

CHAPTER 27

I had known from the start, of course, that the demon's plans involved more than just Father John. The fact that it was producing drugs and distributing them made that clear. It was no victimless crime. Nonetheless, the urgency of the situation bubbled up in me, and I rested my head in my aching hands.

"So we are to just wait?" I asked Jim.

"Sometimes, that's all we can do, Cass." Jim answered. "That and rest since, until we have a plan of action, there's nothing we can do but stay ready. Sometimes, it's a whole lotta hurry up and wait."

I sighed but nodded. While I wouldn't—couldn't—allow the demon's threats to determine my actions, that didn't mean I was any less bothered by them. Eirlas and Dust could be beset at any moment for all I knew, and while I still wasn't entirely sure what I thought of Eirlas, I knew I didn't want him harmed for mere connection to me. Whatever he had done, he had been through enough hell already and didn't need more.

While Jim made his phone calls, I dragged myself into the bathroom and leaned over the sink, splashing cold water on my face with my bandaged hands to try and clear my head. The cold and damp made my palms ache, and the chill didn't help my thought process much, either. I then shut the door and sat on the closed toilet lid. I needed a few minutes to myself to make some sense of all of this.

I drew a shaking breath and closed my eyes, lowering my head and reaching out in wordless prayer. The Father may have had little enough liking for me after my fall, but my taint shouldn't have affected His care of the others, so I prayed for their safety and well being, as well as for my own understanding. I wasn't audacious enough to request blessing, but if nothing else, I could ask for the strength to do His bidding and protect His children.

I don't know how long I sat there in prayer, but eventually, Jim tapped on the door. "Everything all right?"

Straightening, I nodded. "Yes." I stood and opened the door. "I just needed a moment to myself."

Jim backed away from the door to let me pass. "I made some calls. So far, there aren't any other deaths connected with the Clean Sweep project, but that doesn't mean much. Several of the partners Father John had collected dropped the project after he died, one other transferred to a different church somewhere in Maryland, and one had a stroke and has been in the hospital. The project is dead in the water. So... my guess is the demon knew Father John was the heart of the whole thing."

"It makes sense they would go after the one whose work held it together." I nodded. "Tactically, I understand it."

"Yeah." Jim sighed. "Father John was the lynch pin of a lot of things around here. Without him, I have concerns for the future of a number of the programs at the church, but we'll just have to keep our heads down and keep moving forward."

"We should get ahold of Dust and Eirlas. They should not be out there alone, given what just happened." I leaned against the door frame and rested my head to my arm. "They are unprotected."

"Just how dangerous is this, Cass?"

I grunted. "I will do what I can to bless them. I may be able to provide them with something to help protect them against possession, but..." I lifted my head and looked down at Jim. "If they are attacked, I am uncertain of the outcome."

"Uncertain of the outcome," he repeated, a wry smile tugging up one corner of his mouth. The smile didn't reach his eyes. "Is that your way of saying we're screwed?"

"Screwed?"

"Uh..." Jim rubbed the back of his neck and actually blushed. "It's a saying. In this context, it means that there's nothing we can do about this, and we're going to end up hurt."

While I didn't want to alarm him unnecessarily, I shrugged once. "I do not know what I am capable of anymore. If I had the full force of my Grace, the fight would be easy. With how things are now, I am uncertain. Our best bet is to meet at the church and stay together. I know that will make what we planned to do more difficult, but I feel it may be our safest option. Should the demons gain control of one of us, it could cause unbelievable difficulty."

"I'm not sure I'd call it unbelievable." Jim grunted and fished his phone out of a pocket. "I'll call the others."

I let him make the calls and stayed where I was standing, flexing my bandaged hands as I tried to feel out what power I had left. Unlike mortal magic, Grace is more or less the force of the soul. Even humans have a small amount of it. That is one of the reasons some humans are able to force demons out through prayer and ritual. The ritual augments and binds the Grace of those participating together into a powerful enough force to push a demon out of someone. It isn't easy, but it is possible.

Ritual magic, I have since learned, more or less relies on the ritual to do the heavy lifting. The symbols, the rites, and the faith in them all have power, and they are what gives rise to the effect. It's sort of like the way a guitar amplifier makes the sound of a guitar louder. More can be accomplished with less. Of course, it also requires extensive knowledge of the rituals themselves. If you perform one incorrectly, it can have disastrous consequences. The rites performed by the church to drive out demons all have such power, though many of them have become weaker over the years since so few believe in the truth of them. Even fewer still know all the steps that must be taken and in what order.

As an angel, I have the raw power to bypass the need for a ritual in most things that would require Grace. Or at least, I *had* the raw power. I wasn't entirely certain what the limits to what I possessed now were, and I wasn't looking forward to testing them if what had happened to my hands when I'd healed that man was any indication. For the first time since my fall, I felt my lack of weapon keenly. What I would have given for the sword I once wielded as a guardian of the gates of Heaven.

I focused on the present and shook myself just as Jim hung up the phone. "We're converging at St. Mary's," he said.

"Good. Do you have a weapon of some kind I could use? I would prefer an edged one—maybe a large knife if you have some such thing—but I am willing to work with any of them."

Jim chewed over the thought for a moment. "I have guns, but I'm not sure that would be wise. Do you even know how to use one?"

I laughed involuntarily, which earned me a scowl from Jim. "I am sorry." I waved a gauze-covered hand. "I sometimes forget that you do not know much about me." I splayed my fingers. "I have no experience with firearms, but there is no doubt in my mind that I could use one."

Jim gave me a dumbfounded look. "Explain?" he drawled, making a "go on" motion with his hands.

"I was created to be a warrior. A guardian to the gates of Heaven itself. Angels are given certain capabilities and knowledge based on their designation. For example, those angels who provide healing and succor have an intimate knowledge of the body. They were never taught—they just know. I was built to fight. I am capable with any weapon provided, and if I have no weapon, I can make do with whatever I have access to."

He narrowed his eyes and rolled over to his bed, pulling a 9mm handgun in a case out from under the edge of the bed. Flicking the case open after unlocking the combination, he made sure there were no rounds in the firearm and offered it to me. "Prove it."

I accepted the weapon, felt its weight in my hands, and closed my eyes. Then, with them still closed, I broke the firearm down into its parts as though for cleaning and then reassembled it. It felt natural, as though I had done this thousands of times. I knew each part, how to clean it, what it did, and how it worked, even though I had never before in my life done such a thing. I still preferred swords. But this would do.

When I opened my eyes again, Jim was staring at me, mouth hanging open. I stood and offered the handgun back to him. "I do not know many things about this world, but war? War I know."

He took the weapon and set it in its case. "I... am impressed," he said, shaking his head. "But still, I'd rather we not bring firearms into this. The sound alone would draw attention, and if I give you my gun and something happens, someone's hurt, I'll be arrested, too."

While I could have told him I wouldn't miss, I accepted his point. No part of me wanted to risk Jim ending up in trouble if I had to defend him. "Do you have a knife, at least?"

"That, I can give you." He put the gun back where it belonged and reached into a drawer within easy reach of the bed. Withdrawing a ka-bar in a plastic sheath, he offered it to me. "Carried this when I was in the service. It's important to me. Please take care of it."

I nodded, unsheathing the knife and looking it over. The balance of it felt reasonably good in my palm, and I twirled it, getting a feel for how it moved in the air. "This will do," I replied, sheathing it. "I do not intend to draw it unless it is absolutely necessary."

"As I'd expect with any weapon," Jim said.

"Are the others heading to the church?"

"Yes."

"We should go, then," I said, sliding the knife into my waistband and letting my shirt cover it.

CHAPTER 28

Jim and I left his apartment and mounted up in his van, heading for the church. Something in the pit of my stomach felt tight. Anxious. It could have been, I guessed, just nerves. The demon's threats had rattled me, but I was trying to ignore them as best I could. The bastard had intended on just such a reaction, and I didn't want to play into his hands.

Neither of us had much to say during the trip, and Jim turned on the radio to a rock station to fill the space. I drummed my fingers on the arm rest on the door and stared out the window as I chewed the inside of my lip. With any luck, I was only being paranoid, and the demon had no idea what we were planning, but I knew that was a long shot. If it had come to tell me to back off, it had to know I was up to something. That also meant we were on the right track, at least. Though what—if anything—Mary Beth had to do with the demon and his plans, I couldn't guess.

My head still ached, though the dizziness was gone for the most part. My forearms and hands had begun to itch, which told me they were healing. The wounds, assuming they were no worse than they looked when Jim had changed the bandages, would be gone in the next day.

The drive didn't take us long, even with traffic. The fifteen-minute ride gave me far too much time to think and to worry, however, and when we arrived at the church, I felt a sense of relief. While it wasn't guaranteed, the hallowed ground of the church and cemetery would provide at least some defense against an onslaught.

This time of the evening, the shelter was just finishing its check-in hours, so a few people were milling around outside that entrance. I grunted and shook my head. There were too many. If something went badly... I rubbed a hand across my hair and straightened as Jim turned off the radio and glanced at his phone. "Looks like Eirlas is here. Dust is Oscar Mike."

I frowned in his direction.

"Oscar Mike. Military jargon. Means 'OM' or 'on the move,'" Jim explained.

"As if one language was not difficult enough," I muttered. "We should get you inside. I will stand watch."

"Just one question, Cass," he said, his voice calm.

"Yes?"

"What is that?" He pointed toward a dark, shadowed figure at the edge of the parking lot. Its height suggested to me that it was a beast, not a human, and the ember-like red eyes told me everything else I needed to know.

"A demon. Get out of the car and get to the church." I unbuckled my seat belt and got out, flipping my shirt over the knife handle so I could draw it quickly.

While I kept an eye on the demon on the far side of the lot from us, I watched for other threats. That one could, I well knew, be some kind of distraction meant to keep my attention. Behind me, I heard Jim getting out of the van and cursed the slowness of the technology. While I could have slung him over my shoulder and made a run for it, I couldn't both drag him out of the van and watch for more threats. Also, I doubted Jim would have appreciated being slung around like a sack of potatoes, as Father John would have put it. Instead, I waited, keeping an eye on the watchful, prowling beast while trying to make sure nothing else got the drop on us.

My vigilance bore fruit as a flicker of motion from my right drew my attention. A small, dark shadow darted toward me. It was, perhaps, the height of a child but its body bore no resemblance to one. Bristling with barbs, the almost ethereal-looking demon glared at me with fiery eyes as it rushed us. I didn't have time to draw my knife, so I instead caught it with my hands as it lashed out at me with claws. Given that my arms were longer than the demon's, all it managed to do was sink them into my biceps, raking at me like a horrid, over-sized cat. I hissed in pain and hurled the demon backwards through the mostly empty lot, sending it stumbling.

"Jim?" I asked, not daring to look behind me as I drew the borrowed knife.

"I'm out." He spoke from immediately behind me.

"Start for the church. Stay alert. I will protect you as best I can."

And that's when it all went to hell.

Demons poured into the parking lot, emerging from the gathering shadows of the autumn night. While none of them were big, there were more of them than I could easily face alone. Jim started to make for the church as quickly as he could—which was rather fast, to be honest. I'd never seen him move like that, and had I the time to think about it, I'd have said so. I shadowed him, doing my best to keep the small, barbed creatures off us.

We made it a little more than halfway across the thirty or so yards between us and the doors when there just were too many for me to fend off. I was, by then, bleeding from dozens of small cuts and gashes all over my arms, shoulders, and back from where they had been darting in to swipe at me before fleeing again. I knew they were toying with me, but I couldn't do much about that while also protecting Jim.

Giving up on the idea of him getting himself to the doors, I summoned my wings and grabbed him, yanking him up into my arms as I ran, using my wings to bat the beasts aside as they swarmed us. As soon as we reached the sanctuary, I pulled on the doors and found them locked. Of all the times. Crouching, I sprang upward, beating my wings to try and gain altitude.

For those who don't fly, launching from the ground and gaining air like that is excessively difficult. It's far preferable to start from an elevated position so you aren't just trying to yank against the pull of gravity yourself. The muscles in my back and chest strained as I fought to rise even as the demons grabbed at my legs, tearing my jeans and raking claws down my calves and thighs. I kicked at them and managed to get high enough that they couldn't reach me.

Jim had one arm around my neck. With his free hand, he drew the gun I didn't know he'd brought and pointed downward in the direction of the demon horde and fired.

Despite knowing how to disassemble, reassemble, and operate a firearm instinctively, the sharp roar of it was no less deafening than it had been the first time I'd encountered one. The first shot made me falter a little in my desperate attempt to gain altitude, and the next several left my ears ringing. It hurt being so close to something so loud, but I was nonetheless grateful he'd brought it.

Several of them fell back and away from us as I pulled us free and got high enough that I could land on the one-story roof above the entryway into the church.

"Can they get us up here?" Jim asked, yelling the words.

"Might be able to climb," I called back over the ringing in my ears. "I need to get you inside."

"Back door. I've got the key." He holstered the firearm and fumbled with his keys for a moment while I watched the seething mass of demons below us. It was just dark enough that they looked like something resembling natural shadow if you ignored the glowing eyes and furious snarling noises. I looked toward the shelter, a separate building from the main sanctuary, and saw no one outside. Either they had gone inside or fled, and I was certain the gunshots had been heard. How could they not be? Someone would be calling the police, which would only give those creatures ammunition. If they started possessing police officers, this could get bad quickly.

Unsure of what else to do, I adjusted my grip on Jim and jumped off the lip of the roof, climbing into the air to try and get over the building and around to the back door. With the extra altitude, this was far easier than the frantic escape I'd undertaken a few minutes ago.

The pounding headache that had begun to subside as we'd been driving here came back full force, but I did my best to ignore it. I didn't have time for such things. Dropping onto the ground on the far side of the sanctuary, I mouthed a prayer in Enochian that this would work. I held Jim close to the doors, and the moment he unlocked them, I staggered inside with him.

"They'll burn the building down to get to us," I gasped. "We can't stay in here too long."

"I thought churches were safe!"

"The lesser demons cannot enter the sanctuary. But there's nothing saying they cannot try to force us to come out."

"Put me down. I need to call Dust. And Eirlas. Dust doesn't know what he's coming into."

The back door to the sanctuary led into the area right by the podium, so I set Jim on the edge of the stage to let him do as he needed while I considered my options. The beasts would take whatever targets they could get, but I suspected they were more interested in me than in Jim or the others in the church.

I took a step toward the door, and Jim grabbed my wrist with an iron grip. "I don't think so."

"Jim, they're after me. If I—"

"You're going to shut your mouth, let me make my calls, and then we are going to figure out what to do next together. If they get to you and tear you apart, we won't be better off. Mary Beth will still be missing, and we'll be down our most powerful asset. Don't be stupid."

The words stung, and I frowned at him. "I can fight them better than you and the others can, and the police will be here soon. We cannot stay. They will tear the building down, possess the police officers, and innocents will get hurt."

"The longer you argue with me, the less time I have to make the calls I need to," Jim snapped. He then let go of my wrist and picked up his phone. A moment later, he was explaining to Dust that something had gone sideways and he needed to stay away from the church. Jim said he'd be in contact soon then called Eirlas and tried to figure out where in the church complex he was.

A few moments later, Eirlas burst through the side doors into the sanctuary from the direction of the shelter, looking pale and terrified. "What is going *on* out there?"

"Demons," I said matter-of-factly.

Eirlas went so still, I wondered if he'd turned to stone. "Demons. Real, actual demons?"

I nodded once. "We have to get out of here. I think the cemetery is a better option. It, too, is hallowed ground, but there should be nobody else there this time of night, and they cannot burn it down to find us. It is less sheltered, but at the same time provides better protection. At least against this."

"Then why did you have us meet at the church to begin with!" Eirlas threw his hands up.

"I was not expecting them so soon. Or here. I thought we had more time, but I would have contacted you sooner were I able." I met his frustration with a scowl.

Jim grunted. "How are we supposed to get to the cemetery, Cass? If we walk out the ground floor doors, they'll be on us."

"I can carry you both if we can get to the roof. It is not far."

"You can carry two people at once?" Eirlas looked incredulous, and I couldn't help the wry smirk that appeared on my lips in response.

"I *am* an angel of the Lord."

Jim laughed, though the laughter felt tight and a little hard. "Well, at this point, you're my pack horse, so what's the plan?"

"The belfry," I said, looking upward. "It is the highest place we can get to, but I will have to break some of the shutters to get out."

Jim followed my gaze. "A broken shutter can be replaced. We cannot. Are you sure you can carry both of us?"

"Yes." I didn't even need to consider the question. "I can hold you in my arms, Jim, and Eirlas, if you hold onto my back, I should be fine. Just use caution with motion or you will throw off my balance."

With our plan more or less agreed upon (Eirlas still didn't look like he trusted it), I picked Jim up again and carried him to the back of the stage where the stairs to the belfry lay.

The bell these days was rung by a rope tied to the clapper rather than having the whole bell swing back and forth. It still worked just fine, but it rang somewhat quieter than originally intended, or so Father John told me. The stairs up to the belfry were used rarely these days since a rope hung through a hole in the ceiling that allowed people down in the main body of the church to ring the bell. The stairwell was narrow, and the stairs creaked, and there were no lights in there.

I dismissed my wings until we were where we needed to be. There just wasn't room for them. I adjusted my grip on Jim, telling him to put his arms around my neck, and I carried him with his chest and belly against mine to ensure I didn't crack his head off the wall or anything.

At that proximity, I could feel his heart pounding against my chest as clearly as I could feel my own. For all he was acting calm and was focused, I knew he was afraid. All three of us were. I hugged him a little tighter, wishing I could promise him this would work and that we would be all right.

The narrow stairwell was dark as we ascended, which meant I had to feel my way up. I had been up there only once before when I'd asked Father John where the door led. And he hadn't had me go up here in the dark. Other than the creaking stairs, the only sound I really heard was Jim breathing in my ear and Eirlas muttering something under his breath, though I had no idea what he was saying. The stairs wrapped tightly around the enclosed space, and we had to climb what I guessed were at least three floors' worth before we emerged into the belfry. The church bells hung to my left over the yawning darkness of the tower below. The slatted shutters around the exterior of the belfry let in very little light, so I could almost not see my hand in front of my face despite being outside. I only had any idea where I was because I'd been up here once with Father John.

Closing my eyes, I tried to orient myself and chose a shutter to break out, praying it was the right one. I punched the old wood several times and felt it splinter under my fist, the sharp edges biting into my knuckles. It took several strikes to get it to the point where I could push the shutters out. They creaked and swung open and then fell free of the hole I'd made.

My prayers were answered, and I found myself facing the cemetery. Leaning out a little, I looked down and saw a gathering cloud of demons around the outside of the church. None were trying to get in—they weren't stupid enough for that. But in the distance, I could hear sirens, and I took a slow breath.

"This is it," I said, standing away from the window and looking at Eirlas. "It is too narrow for me to get through with my wings out, so... you are going to have to trust me."

"Wait, wait, wait," Eirlas said, holding up his trembling hands. "You're just going to jump out the window holding us and hope you can right yourself in time before we, oh, I don't know, *slam into the ground?*"

"More or less, yes. We do not have any other options that I know of, and there are more of them out there than there were before. The police are coming, and we do not have much time."

"This is madness." Eirlas was nearly yelling, his voice shrill. "How can we know you even... You're fallen. Couldn't you be one of them?" He pointed a finger at me.

Jim adjusted himself and craned his head around to look at Eirlas. "But they that wait upon the Lord shall renew their strength; they shall mount up with wings as eagles, they shall run and not be weary, they shall walk and not faint."

"I'm pretty sure that has nothing to do with jumping out a fucking window into a mob of demons and hoping a supposed angel doesn't drop you or feed you to them!"

I grit my teeth. "We do not have much time. You can stay here if you like, but either you trust me, or... I do not know what will happen. I am not a demon. I am not evil. I am not going to hurt you. And we do not have time for me to prove it. You can either have faith in me or not. But make your choice swiftly." His lack of belief hurt, but not half so much as the idea of leaving him behind.

Eirlas stared at me for a long time, and then at Jim. He shook his head. "I guess there isn't much choice."

I nodded and looked at the window again. "I am going to climb up onto the ledge. Once I am on there, climb onto my back. Be mindful of where my wings are going to be and hold on." To be honest, I wasn't happier about this idea than they were. It relied a great deal on my ability to have the strength and reflexes I had once had. Were I not fallen, this—as with a great many things—would have been child's play. But as it was, I was somewhat apprehensive even though it was the best option I had. Trying to get across the way to the cemetery on foot through that horde of demons was, at best, suicidal. And staying here with the police coming and innocents in the adjacent buildings wasn't an option.

Without giving myself too much time to reconsider, I stepped up onto the window ledge, wrapping an arm securely around Jim's back and holding him tight to me.

"I have faith in you," Jim said softly in my ear.
That made one of us.

CHAPTER 29

Eirlas stepped up behind me and put HIS arms around my neck from behind, overlapping Jim's grip. I took a slow, deep breath. "Ready?" I asked the two of them as I tried to ignore the worry coursing through me at the idea of leaping.

Jim nodded against my neck, and Eirlas let out a shaky laugh. "As ready as I'm ever going to be for this."

I didn't answer and jumped, kicking off as hard from the window ledge as I could, trying to launch myself out and up rather than down. Pulling out of a dive would've been risky with the extra weight even if I weren't heading toward a collection of demons who wanted to do unspeakable things to us. As soon as we were far enough away from the belfry for me to clear the space, I called my wings out, snapping them open as broadly as I could. Eirlas let out a surprised yelp, and I felt his grip around my neck loosen as he slid backwards.

Damn it, I'd told him to be ready. I reached one hand back and grabbed a handful of what I guessed was his shirt and yanked him back up my body as his flailing interfered with my wings and sent me into a spin. Eirlas couldn't hold on through that, not being a particularly strong man to begin with. He grabbed at my back and shirt, eventually locking his fingers into my belt, which yanked me upright. I grimaced and shifted my focus from him to trying to right myself as a tree on the edge of the cemetery came racing toward us. I had what felt like far too much time to realize I was going to hit it if I didn't find a way to change our trajectory.

The belfry was only a hundred or so feet from the edge of the cemetery, which meant that even with this disaster of an attempt, we'd probably make it to the cemetery. Whether we'd make it over the fence or land without colliding with a gravestone was anyone's guess. And, of course, there was that tree.

It felt like time slowed as I cupped my wings to try and stay in the air and slow our velocity toward the tree and fence. That action caused Eirlas's momentum—which was separate from mine now—to whip my legs forward. I twisted midair, which put my back to the cemetery, and I beat the air with my wings. I felt like a chicken someone had grabbed as I flapped madly and attempted to gain control of our descent. I didn't have much luck, but we didn't hit the tree, and I managed to keep us high enough that Eirlas cleared the fence. Mostly. It caught his heels as we went over it. In a last-ditch attempt, I spun midair and curled myself around Jim to try and protect him from the impact, hoping I'd hit whatever we landed on first.

I landed on my back, as I'd hoped, and slid along the ground before striking the cold, unforgiving granite of a tombstone with the back of my head and shoulders. With them splayed and helter-skelter, my left primary wing caught a different stone and yanked at an angle. Something in it snapped, sending a shock of pain through me. I couldn't so much as cry out in response as I fought the panic that came with being unable to breathe. I released Jim, who rolled off to my side, and tried to force my lungs to remember their job. After a terrifying few moments, I managed to force myself to exhale with a deep groan and was able to draw a breath shortly after that.

When I was able to think again, I pulled myself into a sitting position. The motion made the injured wing feel as though it was being pulled out of its socket. I hissed through my teeth in an effort to not scream. At least we were in the cemetery.

Hallowed ground has many functions, but one of them is preventing lesser demons from treading on it. Sure, a greater demon or archdemon can make themselves enter the space, but it strips them of some of their power. The longer they stay, the weaker they become.

Of course, hallowed ground is more than just a spot someone prays over. It requires specific blessings and, much like the exorcism rite, the process of creating such a space is largely forgotten by the modern world. However, some churches—particularly old ones—have the real thing. And the older the church, the more potent the space. St. Mary's church was almost three hundred years old, or so Father John had told me once. The cemetery had graves stretching all the way back to the Civil War era, which meant it was the real thing. The graveyard had expanded over time, which meant that the most potent space of protection was where the oldest graves lay.

Which wasn't where we were.

I dragged myself to my feet, trying to ignore the pain I felt blossoming everywhere. "Jim, Eirlas. You all right?" I gasped, looking between the two of them.

Jim nodded a little, his eyes still locked on the church. The flood of shadows had shifted and were now seething up against the cemetery fence, snarling and hissing and spitting darkness as they stared at us.

Eirlas, on the other hand, peeled himself off the ground, blood streaming from a cut above one of his eyes. He must have landed hard. "I knew that was a damn stupid idea," he spat. "But at least we made it."

I shook my head. "Not yet. We need to keep going." I looked at Jim. "I am sorry to have to keep hauling you around like this."

He grunted. "Right now, it's what we've got. I'll soothe my pride later. Let's get moving."

I changed positions and clenched my jaw to cut off the growling groans that clawed at my throat. Drawing Jim close to me, I picked him up again and stood, the broken wing flopping uselessly to the side.

Eirlas looked at my wing and then at me. "Cass, you're... you've got bone sticking out. And you're bleeding." His tone softened, and his expression shifted from angry and afraid to worried for me.

"We cannot deal with that now," I said, shaking my head. "We need to get to the oldest part of the cemetery. We will be as safe as we can get there. There is also a vault which should afford us a little extra defense."

Eirlas lifted a hand and walked over, carefully and gently folding the wounded limb. Even as gentle as he was, it still hurt like hell. "I'll carry this. No use having it slamming into things as we move. Or can you just..." He waggled the fingers of one of his hands in a "poof" gesture.

"I can probably banish it for now, but it will not stop the bleeding." It took more concentration than I wanted to admit to, to hide my wings again, and I staggered a little. Maybe I'd hit the ground harder than I thought.

"How does that work, anyway?" Eirlas asked as he put a hand on my shoulder and guided me toward the old part of the cemetery. We all knew where it was—the oldest graves were some of the best tended, though I'd never really known why. Father John said it had something to do with the historical society, but I'd never really understood it.

I tried to figure out how to answer the question as we walked, my legs feeling more and more leaden as we went. "They just... they are more or less incorporeal. But still present. I am not sure how to explain it to you. I can still feel them even when they are not visible."

Eirlas nodded, appearing to accept the explanation as we made our way toward the dubious safety of the vault.

Jim, I noticed, had drawn his handgun again and was watching the area around us as we moved. I was grateful, since the pain I was in was slowing me down. At least I hadn't needed to use more Grace. But now we were trapped here, and I had no idea what to do next.

The gravestones around us gave way from the thick, modern stones with their deep-carved names to stones made of what I could only guess was slate. The details on the stones became finer, too. Images of willow trees were common on the older stones. I could feel it the moment we crossed the threshold into the sanctum of true holy ground, and some of the knots in my chest started to unwind.

The vault wasn't far from where we were, and the three of us made our way to it. The gates were locked with a chain and a heavy lock to which none of us had the key. I sighed and set Jim down for a moment before returning to the door.

"What are you doing?" Jim asked, frowning.

"Gaining us entry. I need both hands." I gripped the chain and pulled. The welds on several of the links snapped, and I bent them apart before setting the chain aside and opening the gate. It screeched in protest but provided no meaningful resistance. When I turned back to pick up Jim again, both he and Eirlas were gaping at me.

I paused. "What?"

"That chain was designed to keep out even extremely strong creatures," Jim explained.

"Clearly not angels," I said with a shrug. I gestured toward the yawning darkness, leaning on the gate. "Go on."

"Also, I could have picked the lock so we wouldn't have to buy a new chain," Eirlas said, but he caught my meaning and descended the stairs while I walked over to Jim and picked him up, holding him close. The movement drew a groan from me, but I tried not to complain—I didn't want them to worry. I was starting to feel a little dizzy.

Jim looped an arm around my neck. "Once we're inside, we have to do something about that wing," he said quietly. "I know you're not human, but you will bleed out if we don't do something. And even if you heal faster and better than we do, it needs to be set."

I grunted. "We will deal with that when we are safe." Carrying Jim, I stepped through the gate and had Jim pull it shut behind us and wrap the chain around it so it looked more or less intact. I then descended deeper into the vault.

CHAPTER 30

The vault at St. Mary's, in the old section of the cemetery, smelled of earth, moss, and the musty scent of unused places. It hadn't housed a body in many, many years, but it was an ideal place to take shelter for our purposes. It wasn't very deep, but we could get far enough in to be away from the door, and a large, carved stone sepulcher in the center of it would block line of sight. It was good enough for now.

I sunk to my knees behind the sepulcher and set Jim down, leaning into the cool stone. It felt good, though I couldn't quantify why or how.

As soon as I set him down, Jim gripped my shoulders and pushed me firmly onto my back. "All right. Manifest your wings, Cass. We need to get the broken one set and the bleeding stopped." His tone was all business, but his hands were gentle, if insistent.

I sighed and moved to a spot on the floor where I had enough space and called my wings out. Eirlas had to hop out of the way, and I would have apologized but a sick swell of pain rolled over me. All that came out was a groan.

"Eirlas, you ever dealt with anything like this before?" Jim asked, pulling out his cell phone and turning on the flashlight to get a good look at what was going on. Given time to really figure out where it hurt, I could tell it was the "forearm" part of my wing, between the elbow and wrist joint. That was all I could tell about it beyond the fact that something was desperately wrong and hurt like hell.

And I would know. Hell hurts.

Eirlas shook his head, features alien in the harsh light of the LEDs. "I saw a lot of knife injuries. Some gunshot wounds. Lots of overdoses, but... breaks like this weren't common. We should get her to a hospital. Looks like she's bled a lot."

Jim sighed. "Wouldn't be safe with those things out there, even if we could get her out of here." He handed his phone over to Eirlas. "Hold this. I'm going to try and at least get things lined up. Also, if you can, try and hold her wing still. This is going to hurt, and it'll only get worse if she flails around."

Eirlas gave me an uncertain look. "I don't think I'm strong enough, but I can try." He sighed. "If Dust were here…"

I grunted. "I will do my best to stay still."

Jim patted my shoulder but didn't answer directly. Instead, he maneuvered himself around to reach where he needed to. Eirlas knelt over me, laying his body across my chest and putting his hands on the uninjured part of my damaged wing. His weight was meager, and I could've lifted him with one arm easily, but I didn't tell him that—he was already worried enough.

Instead, I gripped into his shirt and clenched my jaw.

"On three," Jim said. "One, two…" There was no three. He yanked hard on part of my wing without warning.

My vision went dark and then white burst across it as pain screamed through every fiber of the wing. I must have screamed, but I have no memory of doing so. Instead, I held tight to Eirlas's shirt and devoted every part of my focus to not hurling Eirlas off me or hurting him.

When I could breathe or think again, I registered half-sentences as Jim and Eirlas tried to comfort me. "What… what happened to *three*?" I asked through gritted teeth.

Jim let out a humorless laugh. "It's a dirty trick, I know. But it means you won't tense up." He had stripped off his tee shirt and torn it into pieces, tying them around the break tightly. My guess was he was trying to stop the bleeding. He reached a bloodied hand out and patted my shoulder. "How're you doing?"

"How do you think?" I snapped, letting go of Eirlas, who peeled himself off me. I used my shirt to wipe sweat and tears off my face. The pain was different now, but I didn't have words to explain how other than that. "May I put them away?"

Eirlas frowned. "We're only trying to help, Cass."

I grunted. "I am sorry. I hurt. A lot."

Jim squeezed my shoulder. "I'd leave them out for now. We need to make sure the bleeding stops. Once we know for sure, you can dismiss them." He didn't seem fazed by my foul temper in the slightest.

Taking his phone back from Eirlas, he turned off the flashlight and moved, lifting me up a little so my head and shoulders were in his lap. It was marginally more comfortable than the floor. I then felt Eirlas drape his jacket across my chest, and I realized how cold I felt.

"Do we need to be worried about shock?" Eirlas asked as he tucked the jacket in as best he could.

"I don't know, but we need to figure out our next step. We can't stay in here forever." Jim patted my hair in a soothing manner. "I don't know how long those shadow demons will stay out there. That said, I'd guess we're on the right track if they're after us. Means we're kicking the right beehives."

Eirlas sighed and checked his phone. "Dust still hasn't responded. Either he's busy or…" He trailed off.

I shivered a little while I tried to scrape together my thoughts. "All we can do is pray right now. They will not stay out there forever. At least not the whole lot of them. They will probably leave a few to stand watch once they realize we are not coming out."

Jim continued stroking my hair as we tried to figure out what to do next, and while it did nothing for the pain or the cold I was feeling, it helped a little with the panic that tried to well up in my chest.

"Why didn't you just fight them?" Eirlas asked.

I grunted. "I could have, but it would have required me to use more of my Grace, and I have already spent much today. It was smarter to retreat and try and recover."

Jim explained what happened with the possessed man, and Eirlas let out a shuddering sound in response. "So that's real? They can just… hop in and drive?"

"Some can. Others are not designed to. It is different for each of them. But yes, possession is a thing." The shivering continued, intensifying some.

"You know any magic?" Jim asked Eirlas, frowning.

"Uh… not much. Just what they taught me in grade school."

"Can you do enough to warm your hands?"

He was quiet for a moment before nodding. "Yeah, I can probably manage that. I haven't done any in years, though."

"We've got to get her core temperature up. She's definitely in shock." Jim shook his head. "Thought I left this kind of thing behind in Iraq."

Eirlas closed his eyes and focused, going still for a few moments before he lifted his hands and seemed to almost knead the air in front of him. He then slid his hands under the jacket and under my shirt, pressing them to my belly and lower chest. It was strange to be touched there, but I was in no condition to object.

When Jim asked him why he was, by all accounts, groping me, Eirlas shook his head. "You get the heart area warm, it'll heat everywhere else. I learned that on the streets. Used to keep hot packs in the inner front pockets of my jacket all the time, and it helped keep the rest of me warm. It only does so much, but it's the best I can do. I promise I'm not trying to be weird."

That answer seemed to mollify Jim, and we sat in silence for a while as Eirlas tried to help keep me warm, Jim tried to sort out our next move, and I tried to stay awake.

CHAPTER 31

I don't know how long we sat in darkness with Jim and Eirlas trying to keep me warm as I fought the chill that threatened to overwhelm me, but when time started to matter again and the shivering stopped, I sighed. The shadows outside had deepened to full darkness, but that did little to help me know the time.

"How're you doing?" Jim asked, his voice quiet.

"I am less cold than I was, though I do not hurt less."

He nodded. "You can stop, Eirlas."

Eirlas sagged and slid his hands out from under my shirt, fatigue weighing heavily on him. He checked his phone again, the low light of the screen illuminating his sharp features with a blue cast. "Got a message from Dust. He's bunkered down somewhere. Wants to know if we're all right." His thumbs tapped the screen as he responded.

"Be careful." I lifted a hand. "We do not know for sure that he was not captured or possessed. Do not tell him much."

A deep frown furrowed Eirlas's brow, a sort of desperate anguish. "If he is… what do we do? I can't lose him."

Jim checked on my wing with his cell flashlight. "Looks like the bleeding has stopped. You can put them away, Cass."

I did so and sat up, Eirlas's jacket sliding off me, but I ended up leaning back into Jim's chest as dizziness washed over me from the change in position. Jim caught me and pulled me close as I had done for him since I'd scooped him out of his wheelchair. "Slowly now."

Once I was upright, I rubbed at my face with both hands. "We need to meet with him in person. I will know if he is himself. If he has been taken, then I can drive the demon possessing him out."

With it banished, I could still feel the wing. It throbbed with pain with every move I made, but at least I couldn't hit it on anything, and I wasn't at risk of moving it carelessly. The experience was exhausting nonetheless, and I still felt foggy and confused. "How long has it been?"

Eirlas glanced at his phone. "A couple hours. We're pushing eleven."

I rose, leaning on the sepulcher for balance. "I am going to see if the horde has moved on or not. Then we can make decisions."

"You're injured and obviously not feeling—" Eirlas grabbed my arm and stood.

I cut him off. "You are right, but neither you nor Jim could handle a direct attack from a demon. If one made its way into the graveyard or, worse, was strong enough to withstand the hallowed grounds here, it would be a death sentence for you. I can at least stand my ground if I must." I put my hand over his. "But I am grateful for your concern."

He squeezed my forearm but let go. Jim looked up at me with a stern expression. "Be careful. Be smart."

"I am not going far. And I will be both of those things." I took a few breaths to steady myself before leaving the safety of the back of the vault and returning to the door.

After unwinding the chain from around the bars, I stepped out into the calm orderliness of the graveyard. It had begun to rain while we were underground, tucked into the safety of the earth. I hated rain. The feel of it. The scent. While, on a logical level, I knew it was pleasant enough, I could only associate it with my fall. It had, after all, been the first thing I'd ever felt.

The cold air brought back the chill I had just fended off, and I rubbed my arms briskly to try and stay warm as I looked around. Everything looked as still and calm as the graveyard had ever been. Back toward the church, I neither heard sirens nor saw evidence of activity. Taking a steadying breath of the cool evening air, I strode off toward the fence, pausing near where I had struck the ground and, I now realized, the edge of one of the grave markers. I had left a smear of blood on the surface that the rain was only just beginning to wash clean.

Beyond the obvious evidence of my less-than-graceful landing, I saw nothing lurking in the darkness, and more importantly, felt nothing. If there were demons out there, they were far enough away that I could not sense them. My ploy, awkward and injurious as it had proven, had worked. At least for now.

I returned to the vault and stepped inside, shivering a little again. "They appear to have left for now," I said. "We should get moving while we have the chance. Where should we meet Dust?"

Jim sighed as I rounded the sepulcher, looking up at me. "I'd normally say the church, but given the circumstances, it isn't as safe as I could hope."

Eirlas frowned. "These demons are likely following us and know our haunts and patterns, right?"

I nodded.

"When I was on the run from the police, it was similar. So the key here will be to go to a place we are not expected. Preferably using means that aren't common for us."

Jim grunted. "I will need to either get my wheelchair back, if they haven't destroyed it, or get another. As much as I appreciate Cass's help, not having her hands free if we get into a fight isn't doing us any favors."

Where would I go that was uncommon for me? How would I get there? I leaned against the wall and rested my head to it, trying to get my exhausted, foggy mind to function as it should. Of course, the reality was that just about anywhere beyond the church, the park near the church, and Jim's home were well outside the realm of where I typically went. So that part was simple enough. I just didn't know enough places to come up with much of an answer. "How far away is New York?"

Both Jim and Eirlas gave me utterly dumbfounded looks.

"I have never been to New York."

Jim burst out laughing, and Eirlas joined him. They continued for a good few moments until Jim wiped his face. "Cassiel... that is a whole other state. Several hours away. As much as that may be a place they wouldn't think to look for you, it wouldn't be helpful to our cause."

I crossed my arms and tried to ignore the sting of my ego. "Oh."

"Let's start by seeing if my wheelchair is still in one piece," Jim suggested. "Can you lift me, or is it too much?"

It was, perhaps, a foolish sense of wounded pride that drove me to raise an eyebrow at him and scoop him up. For all he wasn't that heavy, he wasn't wrong. I was seriously compromised. I managed, but it wasn't easy, and from the look Jim gave me, I could tell he knew.

Eirlas frowned at me and then out toward the graveyard. "You're sure they're gone?"

"As sure as I can be, yes." I nodded and carried Jim to the doors. He pushed them open ahead of us with Eirlas closing them again and wrapping the chain to try and keep the doors shut.

"Of course it would be raining," Eirlas grumbled, sticking very close to my back as we retraced our steps toward the church.

When we reached the fence, Eirlas hung back a little ways, his eyes wide and shoulders tense. I paused and looked back at him. "You are safe. Even wounded, I have enough strength to protect you. I promise you."

While the tired, hurting, scared part of me wanted to snap at him, I knew he was terrified with good reason. He had only been delivered proof-positive evidence of angels earlier the same day and then been delivered obvious and vicious proof of demons. Not only that, he had to be cold, exhausted, and probably battered from our landing just as I had been.

Eirlas seemed to accept my words, swallowing hard and nodding. "If I can't trust an… actual angel, who can I trust, I guess. Walk by faith and not by sight and all that."

I nodded and took a deep breath, praying silently that I wasn't leading him into a trap.

CHAPTER 32

I climbed over the fence—which stands at about shoulder height to me—and the three of us got Jim over next, Eirlas nimbly hopping it last. Once we were over, we all stood silent for a long while, waiting, each watching the shadows with similar paranoia. When nothing ate our faces for us, we scuttled across the parking lot to where we had left Jim's chair.

Since it had no longer contained their prey, the demons had left it unheeded. I settled Jim into it again, and he released a sigh of relief.

"Well, no sense staying here. We can talk and drive." He headed for his van and loaded up. Eirlas and I piled in after him, breathing a sigh of relief as he got us out of the parking lot. A strange, hollow sensation filled me as I realized I was relieved to be *leaving* the church, but I pushed it aside, not willing to dwell on that at the moment.

"First thing we need to do is get some coffee. Going to be a long night, and we could all use something warm in us." Jim navigated through the Boston traffic with ease, probably heading for a 24-hour Dunkin's, were I to guess.

Despite the medical care Jim had provided, I still hurt terribly, and the headache I thought I had escaped earlier returned, creeping up the back of my neck into my head to make a nest between my temples.

Focus, Cassiel. What is the next step? I rubbed at my forehead, letting out a slow breath. The next step was to meet with Dust and verify he hadn't been possessed. I hoped.

After that?

"Eirlas, did you ever identify the person we should talk to?" I asked, closing my eyes. After having been alone and in quiet for so long of my life, too much input tended to overwhelm me. And right now, with the pain I was in, the fatigue, and the fear, trying to track the movements of the people on the street around us was too much.

"Yes," Eirlas answered. "I was going to tell you when we all met up, but things went all to hell before I could."

"Right. So the plan does not need to change. We just need to find them, pick them up, and interrogate them."

"What about Dust?" Eirlas sounded concerned, verging on angry. As if I'd forgotten about him. "We can't just—"

I held up a hand, forestalling him. "I am not suggesting we leave him out of this. And if he has been possessed, then we will deal with it. I will deal with it. I will not leave him out there alone with them. You have my word. But we must not let this deter us from our focus."

The promise seemed to mollify him for now. I didn't have the heart to tell him that Dust may well be lost permanently, or worse, if the demons really got to him. However, I prayed that wouldn't be the case. "Jim, can you think of anywhere we could meet Dust that is out of our usual spots? I need somewhere somewhat private. If he has been compromised, I will need to exorcise the demon, and that may turn messy. I would rather have as few people around as possible."

I could hear Jim scratch his chin, his nails grinding against the stubble he had there. "Closest thing I can think of is the old zoo. It's been closed for ages now, and so far as I know, it hasn't been turned into anything."

"Zoo?" I asked, finally opening my eyes again and looking at him.

"Ah... a place you go to see animals who don't live where you do. They often try and help protect species that are in danger of dying out and teach people about them." Jim glanced at me as he explained, but mostly kept his eyes on the road. "Though we'll get in trouble for trespassing if we're caught there."

"It should not take long. Would this... zoo... be adequate to hold and talk to someone if we need to?"

"Cass, that isn't a good idea. If someone sees my van there, I could get arrested, or worse. It's not exactly a private place. I just suggested it because, if something happens with Dust, there probably won't be anyone in the immediate area. And it's not a place any of us would typically go that I know of."

Eirlas cleared his throat. "Just be careful down there. We may be lucky, but... that place is used for dogfighting these days, so..."

Dogfighting. It meant more than it sounded like. One of the more common underground sports that draws crowds and betting is pitting therianthropes against each other, hence the name "dogfighting". Given how quickly they heal and how well, the therians can have brutal, body-breaking fights multiple times in a week. For some of them, more than once a night.

While therian-only leagues of more mainstream sports, like MMA, exist, dogfighting lacks the rules and structure those sports provide. Instead, it tends to be a no-holds-barred bloodbath. Sometimes even to the death. Eirlas explained it to Jim and I as we drove, and I could almost feel something in Jim hardening as he listened to Eirlas talk.

The notion of anyone doing that to themselves willingly made me feel vaguely ill, and when Eirlas told me many of the participants weren't so willing, that sickness turned to anger. There was nothing I could do about it, of course, but that didn't lessen my revulsion and fury.

Jim bought the three of us coffees, and Eirlas texted Dust to let him know to meet us at the zoo.

The Blue Hill Zoo sat in a large park at the very southern edge of Boston adjacent to Pine Tree Brook and just off the Blue Hills Parkway. The gates out by the road had once been chained shut, but I'd seen that they'd been torn apart when we drove through. When we pulled off the street and followed the short drive into the large, empty parking lot, I took a slow breath. No cars filled the space, and at this time of night, the darkness felt rather complete compared to the rest of the city.

Beyond us, the zoo's turnstiles had been gated and locked with a chain that was newer than the rest of the rusting hulk of the visible structures that crouched in the shadows as though waiting to devour us. It would have looked far less ominous if there were light.

The desolate, empty place gave me a chill I couldn't quite explain, and while we were dealing with actual demons, the zoo gave me pause. There was something about it that felt wrong. Sinister somehow. Not demonic in the way I was used to, but something just as dark.

I got out of the van with Eirlas while Jim elected to stay behind in case we had to make a fast getaway. He kept the engine running and sipped at his coffee while we waited. After what felt like an eternity, a pair of headlights appeared, following the path of the driveway to the parking lot. I had already been tense, but now I nearly vibrated with nervous energy. Needing something in my hands that felt like a weapon, I unsheathed the knife Jim had loaned me.

He must have caught the shine of it in the headlights because Eirlas looked at me. "What the hell is wrong with you?" he snapped. "This is Dust, not some... some demon!"

I grunted. "We cannot be sure until we are sure. And that might not be Dust for all we know."

"It's his truck." Eirlas stepped past me as the truck pulled into a parking space.

Owing to the need to accommodate some of the larger races, some of the vehicles on the road were bigger and more powerful than your average sedan. Dust's truck was one such beast, and it growled as it pulled up near Jim's van. I couldn't tell who was inside, but the engine turned off, and the car door opened.

"Cass? Eirlas?" I recognized Dust's voice. "You all good?"

Something in his tone struck me, making my gut tense and churn, and I grabbed Eirlas's shirt as he tried to walk toward Dust. "Good enough. How are you holding up?" I asked, yanking Eirlas behind me despite his vocal protests.

"Great. You wanted to talk?" Dust lingered behind his open door.

With the lights of his truck still on, I could only see a silhouette and the general shape of him if I squinted against the light. "We need to figure out what our next step is. How we move forward from here."

"The next step, huh?" He laughed, a low, grating noise. Eirlas stepped up behind me, finally realizing what I had sensed. "The next step is to end this bullshit, angel." He lifted a gun from behind the door and fired.

CHAPTER 33

I grabbed Eirlas and more or less hurled him toward cover behind Jim's truck as I felt something strike my left arm, as though Dust had thrown a rock at me. Then I did the dumbest thing I could think of: I ran straight at him.

Maybe he wasn't expecting it. Maybe he couldn't believe I was being that stupid. Maybe he fired and missed. I didn't really register the details of what happened until I reached the door and slammed it into him, knocking Dust into the truck and the gun out of his hand. It skittered across the pavement, and Dust let out something like a roar, pushing back against the door pinning him partially in the truck. When that did him no good—I had the better leverage—he drove a fist into the window, shattering it. I reeled back a little but didn't let up. Keeping him pinned there was about the best I could do.

I didn't want to hurt Dust if he was still in there—still himself—but I couldn't just let him maul me. That said, when Dust reached through the broken window and grabbed my head, trying to slam it into the remains of the destroyed safety glass, I turned it, trying to throw the hand off. No such luck, given that his hands were so big. He jammed my face into the shards of glass and ground my cheek into them.

Despite the new and different pain that poured through the raw nerves, I lashed out and put a hand on him. Instead of fighting, I pulled on my Grace. White fire wrapped around my hand where it contacted his arm, and Dust howled in immediate and sudden fury and surprise. In a frantic motion, he pushed me into the door frame harder. It felt like my skull would burst with the pressure of it.

In reality, I had never done an exorcism before. I understood how, but I had never actually *done* it. And trying to do something you've never done before while your head is being squeezed between an orc's hand and a car door is not a circumstance I'd suggest trying out new skills. But other than hurting him, or killing him, I didn't see any other choices.

My voice raw, I more screamed the Enochian invocation than said it as I poured Grace into my hand, and from my hand, into Dust. I didn't know if it would work if the words weren't enunciated clearly, so I did my best. The syllables flowed over my tongue like water, striking the air with the power of a newborn star. Just saying them took strength I didn't know I had, and as I spoke, the world faded away, leaving nothing but the words, my voice. It grew easier to speak as the distractions vanished, leaving me alone with my prayer.

Jim told me later that he didn't know what happened. He and Eirlas saw Dust grab me and us tussling through the broken window. He had been getting ready to try and figure out how to help when everything went white and far too bright to look at. He had to close his eyes and cover them with his hands to block it out, though the light vanished just as quickly a moment later.

It felt much longer for me.

When I'd finished the invocation, Dust collapsed, dropping to his knees and sliding out of the truck onto the ground. This meant he was no longer crushing my head, too, and I pulled away, dropping back several paces and trying to take stock of everything. I felt numb more or less everywhere and was vaguely aware of something warm and wet covering my face and left arm. That, and I was so exhausted, my eyes blurred.

Jim called out behind me, but with my pulse so heavy in my ears, I had no idea what he was saying. I staggered some but grit my teeth, waiting to see if the exorcism had taken. The demon inhabiting Dust hadn't been a powerful one. It couldn't have been, or it would have put up much more of a fight, but that didn't mean it couldn't pull some nasty tricks.

Dust clambered to his feet, holding his head. His words were a low, growling mix of syllables, but he made no move to attack me. Or anyone else. Why couldn't I understand what he was saying? I frowned, shaking my head a little, trying to clear it. The motion caused the world to swim around me. My perspective shifted, and then everything went black for the second time that day.

───────────

I woke up in the back of Jim's van. Someone was sitting on the floor with me, and we were in motion. Pain rolled over me in a sickening wave, and I tried to sit up. A large hand pushed me flat again, and I didn't have the strength to resist. "You need to stay still."

I recognized Dust's voice and relaxed some, lifting my right hand to touch his. The effort took more out of me than I wanted to acknowledge. "You are all right?"

"Yeah, I'm okay. You're not, but... Shit. I'm sorry, Cass." His voice tightened, and he cleared his throat before continuing. "I couldn't stop it. I knew what was happening, but... I couldn't make it stop." I heard the tears even without seeing them.

That is a common aspect of demon possession and one of the reasons it does so much damage. Being trapped in your head, watching as the *thing* that has taken over destroys everything you care about does a number on a person.

"It's okay. I know. I know." I squeezed his hand and closed my eyes, swallowing. "Listen. If you were aware, what do you remember? It might be important."

"I told Jim already. I..." He took a deep breath. "I was out looking for a place to enact our plan. I'd hit a few locations I'd thought of, but I was up north of town when it got me." His voice shook again, and I squeezed his hand, waiting. If there was one thing Jim and Father John had taught me, it was that sometimes, all you needed to offer a person was space and patience. It was something they'd given me in spades, and right then, I knew it was what Dust needed.

"It took me somewhere off the tracks near Andrew Square. There were a bunch'a people there. It looked like some kind of drug lab or something. There were people all hunched over beakers and stuff. The... the demon was reporting to its boss, I think. Telling 'im that they'd grabbed me and were going to try and use me to kill you. We hung around there for a while before the call came in to get down to the zoo. Mary Beth was in there. I saw her working with something. Poor thing looked at me like she thought I'd help her, and all I did was laugh. It did. I don't know. It. Me. I couldn't tell the difference entirely.

"They knew we were looking for a BHK member to get information since… what's in my head was in the demon's. So that plan's down the tubes. You know the rest. Jim's got us heading to Andrew Station to see if I can pinpoint where I was. Then he wants to call the cops on the place."

"No." Adrenaline surged through me, and I sat up, groaning and blinking a few times. The pain was worse when I sat. My arm pounded along with my heartbeat, as did my head. "If there are demons in there, the police will get slaughtered or, worse, possessed." I forced myself to look around and realized Eirlas was up front with Jim. There was something tight around my left arm where the pain was radiating from, and I looked down to see someone had wrapped gauze around my bicep. "Just point the place out to me. I will finish this."

Dust opened his mouth as though to argue, then closed it again. He was silent for a minute but nodded. "Yeah. I was gonna say there's no way you're able to do that, but… I kind of have proof otherwise." He studied my face, and I imagined I looked like death. I certainly felt like it. "You sure you're up for this?"

"No." I couldn't lie to him. "But nobody but an angel or a Heaven-touched could face this and have even a ghost of a chance of handling it. And right now, I am what we have." The side of my head felt like it was on fire, but the bleeding had stopped. Honestly, given the events of the day, my entire body felt like one raw nerve, and everything hurt.

For all my brave words, I knew I wasn't going to come back out of that drug lab, no matter what happened. If I won the fight, at least, I could free Mary Beth and stop whatever plans the demons had for the drug they were manufacturing. If I lost, it would no longer be my problem.

CHAPTER 34

We arrived at Andrew Square around midnight, and Jim parked at the side of the road. He turned his seat back to face the passenger seats behind him and sighed. He must have heard us talking, and while he hadn't said anything about it, I doubted he liked the idea of me walking into a demon-infested drug lab alone. I didn't blame him. I didn't like it, either. Eirlas's seat didn't turn like Jim's did, but he craned around to look back at us.

"I hate this plan," Jim said with a raw hardness in his voice I hadn't heard from him before. "I absolutely fucking hate it."

I blinked. I didn't think I'd ever heard him swear.

"But I don't see any better alternatives." He sighed, eyes meeting mine. He knew this was probably a one-way trip. "You're right. The police aren't going to be enough for this. But you're not going in alone, Cass. You can fight them, but there might be innocents in there who'll need help getting out before everything goes to hell. That's where the three of us come in. We started this together; we're ending it that way." Jim glanced at the other two. "We're going in hot, but let Cass handle the demons."

Eirlas nodded, his face pale but eyes hard. "What do we have for weaponry?"

Jim pointed at Dust and then down under his seat. "Reach under. Got a case."

Dust did as he asked and pulled out a long, black case from under the seat. Jim leaned forward and flicked some dials set into the front of it before opening the latches to reveal a shotgun and handgun, both gleaming with oil and good care. "Got these and the knife Cass is carrying. Shotgun's mine. Dust, I want you carrying the handgun."

A heavy frown covered Eirlas's features. "What about me?"

"You weren't military trained like Dust and I were," Jim said, shaking his head. "I know you've used a gun before, Eirlas, but this is a little out of your depth. Besides, we need someone who can help people get out of there. Of the three of us, you're the least intimidating, and if we've got terrified people in there, having a friendly face will help more than another gun. Dust, do you remember the layout?"

Dust nodded. "Sort of. Some of it. You got some paper?"

Jim produced a notebook and pen and handed it over, and in the dim haze of the dome light, Dust did his best to sketch out what he remembered the layout being. He said it looked like some kind of industrial building, and it was right on the tracks. The whole place was outfitted with ramps to move heavy cargo around, and the lab was on the main floor of the place where—he guessed— old machines had once sat.

I listened, trying to prevent the fear that had started building in the pit of my stomach from becoming overwhelming. Dust and Jim discussed the best points of entry, and I closed my eyes. I didn't have much to add to their conversation at the moment. Instead, I prayed harder than I had since Father John's death. I begged the Father to protect them. And to protect the innocents in that building. I asked that Mary Beth be safe and be there so we could get her out. I asked that He give me the strength to do this.

I hadn't told them I didn't think I had enough Grace to fully smite something. I hadn't told them I could barely exorcise one demon, let alone multiple, and face down a moderately powerful one. Jim might have guessed that I was expecting a one-way trip, but I didn't think telling the other two would be helpful.

Jim's pronouncement that we had a plan drew me from my thoughts. I opened my eyes again and looked at the map while Jim pointed at various points on it. "We enter here and make our way down onto the main floor this way. It's the fastest way in. As soon as we get there, Eirlas starts pulling people out and sending them toward the front where we've cleared. Dust and I will cover that. Cass, you handle the demons."

Like it was nothing. *Oh, Cass, you handle the demons. It'll be fine.* Dandy. Just perfect. "All right. Do we know where this place is yet, or is this still all guesswork?"

"I don't know exactly where it is, but I'll recognize it when I see it, I think." Dust rubbed the bridge of his nose. "I know it's north of here. On Dorchester, maybe?"

"All right. Eirlas, Dust, switch seats. I'm going to get us on the road. Cass, just close your eyes and rest until we figure this out. We'll need you as ready as you can get for this once we've identified our target."

Jim turned his seat forward again, and Dust got out to let Eirlas take the place he'd been in. He then walked around the passenger door and got in. He was far too big to move around inside the vehicle much even with the back of it mostly open for wheelchair access.

Eirlas settled on the seat near me where I was on the floor, and I sighed, resting my head to the door. Nobody spoke while Jim pulled away and drove. I lost track of time and closed my eyes until Dust paused and pointed. "Left here. That's it. I recognize the building."

Jim turned, and I felt the van slow as he drove past it. "You're sure?" he asked.

"Yeah, I'm sure."

"Can't get in there from this side. It looks like there's an access road back that way, though," he grumbled. "I'm going to have to turn around."

Several more minutes of tense silence passed as Jim found a place to turn around and tried to find a way onto the access road. I closed my eyes again and focused on my breathing. While I could take a lot of pain before dropping, I was at the edge of my limits and knew it. To push further meant doing myself serious harm and, honestly, I knew that's what this was coming to. Using my Grace would help, but I could only sustain it for so long, and my body would fail pretty quickly once I did. As I said: one-way trip.

"This is it." Dust's voice came out a hard growl, and I opened my eyes to look.

With it so late, the buildings around us were dark but for the odd security light and street lights around us. Jim had parked as far away from the building we were after as he could, pulling into a space behind another industrial building. A few scattered vehicles sat in the lot down the way, but there were no signs of life I could recognize. The area we were in sat adjacent to the railway tracks, though they were offshoots of the main line, probably used for loading and unloading into the industrial buildings that surrounded them.

The squat building Dust had identified was a single floor and mostly comprised of a rusting warehouse-like metal building that had once been white, I guessed. Attached to it was a smaller section that Dust had said he thought housed offices. While the fastest route would've been the main doors to the working floor, they were closed, and I doubted knocking on them would gain us entry. Besides, it looked like they were rusted shut.

"In through the office. We use any furniture we can as cover. Get the innocents out and send them back toward the van if possible. For all we know, this lab could blow sky high when the shooting starts. Which... honestly might be in our favor. They won't want to blow themselves up, either, so less likely they'll take a shot at us," Dust said.

"We can't know for sure," Eirlas said. "We don't know what's in it. So... just be ready for anything, all right?"

"Makes me wish we had a mage. Could just hurl ice at 'em and call it a day." Dust grunted.

"Makes me wish we had a lot of things. Including backup," Jim replied. "But I suppose having a literal angel with us will have to do. One more thing before we go..." He looked between all of us and lifted his hands, reaching out to each of us.

The four of us held hands and bowed our heads, our sweaty palms and shaking fingers reinforcing one another. Jim spoke first. "The Lord is my shepherd; I shall not want. He makes me lie down in green pastures; He leads me beside the still waters."

I joined him. "He restores my soul. He leads me in the paths of righteousness for His name's sake."

Dust and Eirlas spoke in unison, the four of us recounting the Psalm:

Though I walk through the valley of the shadow of death, I will fear no evil; for you are with me. Your rod and staff comfort me. You prepare a table for me in the presence of my enemies. You anoint my head with oil. My cup runs over. Surely goodness and mercy shall follow me all the days of my life, and I will dwell in the house of the Lord forever.

"Amen," we said as one.

Saying the words didn't change what we were about to do, didn't change the odds we were up against, didn't change the fact that I didn't know if I had enough Grace to make a difference. However, just the act of saying it aloud, of speaking the affirmation, felt good. I was still in pain, I was still terrified, but at the same time, some part of me down in the pit of my chest felt more settled. More focused.

I had no way of knowing how this was going to turn out, but at least, in that moment, holding their hands, speaking the passage, I felt like I could be at peace with whatever happened.

We held hands for longer than strictly necessary for the prayer, as though we were afraid to let go. When we let go, this had to start. We had to move. This would be no longer just a plan, a theory. It would be action.

Taking a long, deep breath, I released it and let go first, setting off the chain reaction to the others. "Before we go, I should bless you. It is not foolproof, but it should keep them from possessing you immediately if there are any demons without hosts in there."

Heads nodded all around, and I touched each of them in turn, praying over them, and doing what little I could to cover them with my Grace. I didn't have much, and I had to reserve the rest of it for the fight. But I did my best. I wished I had oil to anoint them with. Or much of anything beyond my bare hands. It would have to do.

"Whatever happens out there," I said, "know that I have seen the face of God. You are His beloved children. You do not go into battle alone. And if you die, there is true peace awaiting you." I looked around, meeting each of their eyes in turn. "Be not afraid."

CHAPTER 35

I opened the door to the van and climbed out, and the others joined me. Jim had his shotgun in his lap, and Dust was trying to get his big hands around the handgun. After a few moments, he looked at Jim. "You mind if we switch? Finger's too big for the trigger well."

Jim grunted and made a face, but he handed the shotgun over and took the semi-auto instead. "I should've thought of that."

"You can't think of everything, brother. We ready?" Dust messed with the shotgun some, trying to find the right grip on it. It hadn't been designed for orcish hands, but he made do.

Jim nodded, saying nothing. I followed suit, sticking my hand in my pocket to play with the little cocktail umbrella I kept in there. By now, the paper was ratty and worn from rubbing against my pocket. I'd need to stop carrying it like this soon if I wanted to preserve it, though the idea of leaving it behind created a hole in my heart. This would all be over soon. Father John would be avenged—for what that was worth—and the demons would no longer hurt people.

Eirlas trembled some and looked up to Dust for a long time.

Dust looked down at him, the callow light of the street lamps washing away most colors but yellow. Eirlas then stepped forward, grabbed Dust's shirt, and yanked him down to plant a kiss on the big orc's mouth. It lingered for a long time, and I looked away, feeling as though I'd invaded their privacy somehow by watching.

When they parted, Dust had a stupid grin on his face, as did Eirlas. They didn't say anything, but both of them looked toward the industrial building.

"Let's move." Jim glanced at me. "Cass, you're on point."

I started the long walk from where we'd parked the van. While it was a smart choice to have parked as far away as possible, it felt like it took a hundred years to cross the pavement. Both because of the adrenaline flowing through me and the fact that every step reminded me of the wreckage that was my body. To keep his gun arm free, Eirlas pushed Jim's chair for him, and Dust hovered at their side like a massive junkyard dog ready to bite anything that came at us.

Seeing that change in my friends felt strange, but it just went to show that Jim had been right: we were more alike than I'd really known. At that moment, I knew I could rely on them in ways I hadn't understood before. I knew Jim and Dust were soldiers, but I somehow had put them in a different class from me in my head. I may be stronger than either of them in a physical sense, but I had underestimated both of them badly. I made a mental note to apologize for that when this was all over. If I survived it.

Nothing stopped our approach. If they'd noticed the group walking straight up to the doors, there was no external display of readiness. I had expected to see a few guards, at least. Were they so brazen that they assumed no one would discover this place? Or were they convinced that even if someone did, it would not be a threat? All this said, I did find the office door locked when I tried it. Eirlas shooed me away and pulled out his lockpicks, kneeling in front of the door and fiddling with it for an eternity before he turned the door handle and opened it.

The office beyond was pitch black, and I squinted. Muffled voices and the feel of demonic Blight came from the right, but nothing close enough to worry me. I stalked inside, keeping low as I entered the office area. It wasn't very big, but there was a small lobby with a few chairs scattered around it, one of which I discovered with my shin. Dust hadn't seen this part of the building, so all we could do was guess at its layout. Once everyone was inside, Dust shut the door behind us, and he pulled a small flashlight out of a pocket, clicking it on.

The little waiting room seemed more or less undisturbed. Maybe the demons had no use for it. Not that they were probably entertaining visitors. Glancing at the other three, I nodded once and went for the door into what we hoped was the main office area. This one was unlocked, and Dust's flashlight illuminated a few copiers, desks, and other long-disused office equipment.

Gathering the others close, I spoke in a harsh whisper. "As soon as I break in there, see if you can move a couple of these desks for cover. It is going to get bright when I draw on my Grace. Do not look at me if you can avoid it."

"Kind of knew that already, Cass," Dust said with a low chuckle. "Had firsthand experience and all. We ready?"

Heads nodded all around, and I pulled away from them, heading toward the door to the main production floor. My throat felt dry in a way that couldn't just be the dust in the air, and my head was still throbbing enough to make me feel nauseated. I pushed the pain away as best I could and kept myself focused on the mission. I tested the door handle and found it, too, unlocked.

While I could sense them, being that I was fallen and exhausted, I'd relied on that diminishing my Grace enough that they wouldn't feel me immediately unless they were looking for me. And so far as we knew, they didn't realize I'd exorcised Dust. We were as ready as we were getting.

I threw the door open and walked into the next room, drawing on my Grace to send white fire licking up my body. Despite resembling flames, however, my Grace wasn't true fire, so I doubted it could ignite any gasses in the lab. At least, I hoped it wouldn't. If I'm completely honest with myself, I didn't really think about it much when I did it. The effect was more to surprise and confuse any demons beyond. People shouted, throwing their hands up to cover their eyes.

Dust's layout proved to be pretty true to life, and I found myself on the factory floor with people all around me. Most of the people in the room threw themselves back and away from the tables they'd been hunched over, working. A couple of them let out inhuman roars and reached for weapons. They were where I turned my focus.

Adrenaline poured through me in a wild rush, and I vaulted one of the lab tables, scattering vials and equipment, in pursuit of the nearest possessed. I registered them as a woman with ink-black skin, pale blue hair, and pointed ears. A svartalf probably, though her species was an afterthought as I reached her. She was just lifting a gun to fire at me when I hit her, and we both went down in a heap.

Much like with Dust, time felt like it almost stopped as I performed the exorcism, and I lost awareness of anything around me. Nothing but the rush of Grace and my own voice filled my awareness as I hurled the demon free of the woman before the others had cleared their guns from their holsters. The demon, a dark shadow like a plume of smoke, howled and vanished.

There were two other possessed in the immediate vicinity, but a presence at the far end drew me. Called to me. I recognized it. The same presence that had been there when Father John died. That I'd seen outside Jim's apartment. The archdemon.

What had drained me so much last time only filled me with more focus and purpose now. The act of exorcism felt right. Just. Good. I left the svartalf woman on the ground, breathing but stunned, and stood. Some part of my mind registered the harsh crack of gunfire and the sound of yelling, but the rest of me felt *alive* and was reveling in it. Even the pain I was in had faded so far into the background, I barely noticed it. My hands still itched and burned now and then, and my wing ached, but none of it threatened to overwhelm me.

Instead of charging toward the archdemon immediately, however, I took a slow breath and tried to center myself. I was here for Mary Beth and the other innocents. That had to come first. I could hear Eirlas calling out to them, telling people to come his way, that he'd get them out. He sounded so far away.

I recognized her hair first. Mary Beth looked hollow, frantic, and horrified. She rushed to Eirlas, arms outstretched. He caught her and held her tight for a moment before shooing her out past him toward where the rest of the innocents were going.

With her safe, my focus changed. My lips peeled back from my teeth in a feral snarl as I ignored everything else happening in the room and headed for my target. I didn't even know the archdemon's name, not, I guess, that it mattered much in the scheme of things. The more I drew on my Grace, pulling it into myself until I felt like a well of pure light, the more the world faded around me. The less I really watched. The less I saw. The only thing that mattered was accomplishing my goal, and my focus narrowed down to that singular point. Even the bellow of gunfire didn't faze me, for all I heard it rolling through the air like sharp thunder.

All at once, I was beside the presence I had hunted for what felt like an eternity, and the archdemon turned its head to look at me, eyes widening. The human guise it wore melted away, leaving it revealed as a smoky, humanoid mass of pure Blight with a pair of burning yellow eyes.

"You," it hissed, taking a few steps away from me, revealing wispy black teeth filling its too-large mouth. Its mouth didn't move when it spoke; its voice filled my ears—or perhaps my mind—without physical involvement. "You should have left well enough alone."

As though to match my own, crimson fire appeared across the archdemon's body, the heat of it causing me to recoil some. "You will die here, fallen. You could have lived. But now? Now you are going to die, and then, when you are gone, I am going to play with those friends of yours. Everyone you care about. Everyone you've so much as *looked at*. I am going to take them apart piece by piece."

"No. You are finished. This is finished. You will never hurt anyone again," I said with absolute certainty. The words were law. I drew the knife Jim had given me and lunged forward, trying to stab the beast, but it evaded me, the smoke slipping away and off to my left.

It struck me, ethereal claws raking my already damaged arm and down my ribs. I cried out as the sharp, burning pain skated across me and twisted, trying to ram my knife into it again. The archdemon must not have expected me to do anything but scream because I sunk the ka-bar to the hilt in its belly. Recoiling, it howled in surprise and pain and tore itself back and away from me. I straightened, and while my shredded upper arm and ribs screamed with pain, even that felt somewhat distant.

That said, regardless of whether I felt it or not, my arm didn't want to respond and hung mostly limp at my side. With my knife out of my grasp, that left me with only my Grace as a weapon. A Grace I knew had to be running low.

Smoke?

The scent distracted me, and I looked around us, realizing that fire was catching the tables and papers and furniture around us. The air was heavy with it. How had I missed that? I didn't even feel the warmth.

Even so momentary a lapse provided the archdemon with an opening, and it was on top of me before I could think, hurling us both into one of the tables. More pain. My ribs this time, I thought. It felt sort of vague and distant, though, and I wrapped my arms around the archdemon. For all its raking and clawing and screeching, I had something it didn't.

Instead of trying to fight it hand-to-hand, or claw-to-hand as the case may be, I hugged it close and reached back into the well of my Grace for whatever was left, pulling it into me as I clutched the demon. Contact with that much holy fire would've made Lucifer himself flinch. Archdemon or not, the beast I held howled in pain and fury, raking at me harder. I knew it was doing damage, and it was probably horrible. Even with the heady rush of power flowing through me, I could feel my body weakening. Slowing down.

I didn't let go.

The howling turned into screams. Or maybe that was me. I couldn't tell anymore. The archdemon's body became smaller the longer I held it, and eventually, it was nothing more than ash spread across me. Or it was gone. I didn't know. By then, all I knew was how tired I was.

My Grace faded, the brilliant white light vanishing. But it didn't get dark. Instead, a rolling orange glow filled my vision. *Oh, right. The fire.* Someone was calling my name. A male voice. I knew I knew it, but I couldn't place it. He sounded upset. Frantic. I frowned a little, trying to look toward it. At that moment, a pair of strong arms yanked me up into a semi-sitting position. More scents. Aftershave. Jim.

He was trying to get me somewhere. Drag me, maybe. I didn't know how. He didn't have legs, but he crawled, belly to the floor, one hand gripping my shirt, which he had wadded up in his hand. The cement felt rough on my back. Cold almost by comparison to the air. I tried to tell him to go. That I was sorry. I tried to tell him everything at once, but nothing came out but blood as I coughed. It tasted awful.

So this was dying. No wonder people feared it. It hurt, and if I'd had the energy, I would have been afraid. But I just didn't have the strength in me to summon the emotion. My eyes began to drift closed when everything stopped.

CHAPTER 36

They never really understand the truth of fire, do they. They heat their homes, roast their meat, but they never truly understand its power." A figure emerged from the raging flames, smoke rolling over him. He wore a white robe that hung to his knees, and a pair of gold wings, visible at his shoulders, rested closed against his back. Despite the flames, his soft, golden hair was free of soot, and piercing, sapphire eyes echoed the color of my own.

"Brother," I tried to say, but the words wouldn't come.

He smiled softly at me and lifted a hand. The pressure on my chest and throat that I hadn't quite registered vanished. "Speak freely, seraph." He lifted a hand, trailing it through a plume of fire and smoke as though caressing it. "That was quite some task you undertook."

I cleared my throat. "Someone had to, brother. I could not just let it continue to harm people. And these people could not have stopped it."

The angel nodded, his smile remaining as calm and unruffled as a force of nature. Which I suppose it was, in a way. "Of course, there are those who might question your choice. You are fallen, after all. You have free will. Why care to help a world that doesn't seem to want you?"

"I am still an angel." The notion of abandoning anyone to whatever plans this demon had made me feel sick in the pit of my stomach, and I shook my head. Or tried to, anyway. It didn't really move. "Even Peter denied Jesus. And He still forgave him."

"Your choice, Cassiel, has gained interest, for even as you have fallen, you have chosen faith. Even cast out, you seek to serve Him rather than fall to the desires of this world. It is a rare feat." The angel walked over, kneeling beside me and reaching out to brush a plume of flame away from Jim in a graceful gesture. "Your prayers have been heard, Angel of Tears. You and your friends will not die today." His shining gaze met mine, and he examined my face closely, squinting some as though trying to see through the skin. "He has work He would have you do."

Even without the fire and the pain and the, well, dying, my head spun. Work? Me? I had fallen. I was rejected. I had failed. And yet… I still had a calling? "It is mine to serve."

The angel stood. "Good. With that decision comes a gift. Your flesh was never designed to hold all your power. It cannot. However, the power you possess, you will gain more mastery over." He lifted a single finger. "But should you use this power wrongly, you will face swift judgement."

I sighed, closing my eyes. I had a purpose. I wasn't forgotten. Even fallen, I wasn't lost. "Thank you, brother."

"It is not me you need to thank. I am but a messenger and watcher. This choice, this calling, you will either answer it with the choices you make or you will not."

"It is… nice, to not be alone."

The angel's smile faded, and he frowned. "Did you not know? I have been with you since you fell. It is not mine to interfere, but… sister, you have never been alone." He looked upward as if hearing something I couldn't. "I have things to attend to. I am Codiel. If you speak, I will hear, but do not expect much for favors. I am limited in my permission to be involved."

He nodded once to me and then was gone, and the flames leaped back into full focus around us. The heat, smoke, pain, and exhaustion returned, and I closed my eyes in the peace of knowing Jim would be all right. As would I.

I woke to the taste of copper in my throat and the sterile, dry flow of oxygen into my nose. My heart tightened as I waited to hear Father John reading the Gospel to me, but it never came. Instead, when I opened my eyes, I saw Dust sitting in the recliner beside me, lying back and asleep so far as I could tell. Eirlas sat on a rolling stool beside him, hunched over his phone. Dust had some bandages around his arms but looked all right for the most part, and Eirlas seemed unharmed.

I must have made some kind of noise because Eirlas lifted his head. A weary smile spread across his face. "Hey… hey, Cass." He set aside his phone and stood up, walking over to hold my hand where it lay on the bed. "You gave all of us quite a scare."

"Jim?" I croaked, realizing my throat hurt. Smoke inhalation, I guessed.

"He'll be all right. Got some burns, inhaled a lot of smoke, but he'll be okay. He's resting in the next room over." Eirlas squeezed my fingers. His gaze darted to the door for a second before he looked back to me. "We got Mary Beth out. She was there. We were right. She was admitted, too. They're keeping her to help her detox; the dealers had her drugged up pretty hard. Well, her and everyone else in there. After that, I'm not sure where she'll go. But I plan on talking to her about staying at the church for a while or going to one of the shelters for young women in her position."

I grunted.

"Listen, the cops are going to have questions for you. They know we were looking for Mary Beth and that her trail led there. Don't say anything about demons or any of that, all right?"

I shook my head. "Water?" Everything hurt, and not for the first time, I wished medicine worked for me. Or liquor.

"I'll ask. You, ah… you were really badly torn up. Like… things hanging out of you bad. So just take it slowly all right?" Eirlas let go of my hand and headed to the door to call a nurse.

As he did so, I lay my head back on the pillow and let out a slow breath. Alive. They were all alive. And beyond that, I had a purpose. I didn't know what work He would call me to do, but I resolved to be ready for it when it came.

I left the hospital over a week later. While my swift healing was notable, it wasn't the most remarkable thing any of the doctors had seen, so the hospital didn't ask too many questions beyond pushing to get me to identify what kind of meta I was. I skirted around the subject as best I could, since I didn't know what in the world to tell them. "Hello, yes, I am an angel of the Lord," seemed like it would bring more trouble than it was worth.

When I returned to the church, Father Demoyne made it very clear I wasn't going to be allowed to stay, but nothing stopped me from visiting since he hadn't banned me from the property. After all, I was a volunteer and had never done anything to warrant barring me from the church campus. That, and Jim, Eirlas, and Dust all threatened to walk out on him if he pushed. He didn't.

Probably the wisest thing I've ever seen him do.

Mary Beth left the hospital after I did. We met in the cafeteria at the church, and she threw her arms around my neck. "Thank you," she whispered, her much smaller body trembling against mine. "I know what you did. No matter what the official story was. Thank you."

I squeezed her and then let her go. "You are blessed, child. Your life is your own, and your father can go pound sand." I'd heard the term from Dust a few times along with vastly more colorful versions that I didn't think would go over well.

Mary Beth smiled, a cockeyed thing. "I'm old enough to make choices on my own, and I've decided to move in with my grandmother. She lives in Florida."

"So you are leaving?" I frowned some. It was a strange sensation to be both happy and sad at the same time.

Mary Beth nodded. "Yeah. The people at the hospital suggested I try finding some better support than my dad. My grandma is really looking forward to having me. She told me she always thought my dad was a deadbeat." She smiled a little up at me. "Here."

She put her backpack down and pulled out a book, handing it to me. "I know you said it was awful, but it's the only thing I have that I can give you." It was the same book I'd seen her reading the last time we'd actually talked. The one with the woman dressed in extremely ineffective armor.

"I am not very good at reading," I confessed.

A look of surprise covered her face. "Well, then this should give you a head start. Everyone should read."

"Thank you."

Dust leaned out of the kitchen, gesturing to me. "Hey! I could use some help in here. Not paying you to…" He stopped and frowned. "Just get in here!"

I laughed. "Looks like I have work to do."

"Looks like," Mary Beth said, shaking her head. "Take care of yourself, Cassiel." She waved to me and picked up her backpack before heading out the door.

Though I never saw her again, I have it on good authority that things worked out well for her in Florida. Something for which I have always been grateful. She deserved better.

The ache of Father John's death never really left me, and I found myself thinking of him as I walked into the kitchen and got to work helping Dust. He would, I thought, may be pleased. The demon I'd slain hadn't probably been the demon that had killed his family, but it was *a* demon. Perhaps one day, I would find that demon in particular and smite it in his name. Yeah, that sounded nice.

What good are angels indeed.

E. Prybylski has been in the publishing industry as an editor since 2009, starting at Divertir Publishing and eventually partnering with her close friend Richard Belanger to begin Insomnia Publishing.

Ever since childhood, E. has been an avid reader and writer of fantasy. The first chapter book she remembers reading is The Hobbit, followed swiftly by most of Anne McCaffrey's Pern series. In high school, she perfected the skill of walking while reading without slamming into anyone. Mostly.

When she isn't reading or writing, E. is an active member of the Society for Creative Anachronism and has a B.A. in European history from SNHU. In addition to her many historical pursuits, E. is a musician of multiple instruments, a cat mom, and a loving wife to her husband, J. E. also speaks out for the disability and chronic illness communities being a sufferer of chronic migraines and Ehlers-Danlos Syndrome.

E's blog is located at ThirteenCentsShort.com

CPSIA information can be obtained
at www.ICGtesting.com
Printed in the USA
LVHW011329080122
707889LV00005B/222